C000050426

A Second Roald Dahl Selection

eight short stories by Roald Dahl

edited and introduced by
Hélène Fawcett
North Westminster Community School, London

with photographs by
Catherine Shakespeare Lane
assisted by Lucie Mayer

Longman

LONGMAN GROUP UK LIMITED
Longman House, Burnt Mill, Harlow,
Essex, CM20 2JE, England
and Associated Companies throughout the world.

"The Swan", "The Boy Who Talked With Animals" and "A Piece of Cake" are from *The Wonderful Story of Henry Sugar*, first published by Jonathan Cape Limited in 1977.

© 1977 by Roald Dahl

"Pig", "The Way Up To Heaven" and "Royal Jelly" are from *Kiss, Kiss,* first published by Michael Joseph Limited in 1960. "The Wish" and "Poison" are from *Someone Like You,* originally published by Secker and Warburg Limited in 1954 and republished by Michael Joseph Limited in 1961.

1953, 1959, 1977 by Roald Dahl

This edition © Longman Group UK Limited 1987.

This edition first published by Longman Group UK Limited by arrangement with Jonathan Cape Limited and Michael Joseph Limited 1987.

Fifth impression 1993

Set in 10/11pt Baskerville Lonotron 202

*Produced by Longman Singapore Publishers Pte Ltd
Printed in Singapore*

ISBN 0 582 22499 3

The Publisher's policy is to use paper manufactured from sustainable forests.

Contents

Contents

Introduction

Roald Dahl is one of very few authors who write successfully for both children and older readers. You can start reading his stories when you are quite young, or at least listening to them, and just keep on enjoying them as you grow. In fact, you can grow up with Roald Dahl – a comforting thought? Maybe.

While his stories for children are "marvellous" and "fantastic", these for older readers are much more grotesque and gruesome. No witches or twits or giant peaches, but poison, pigs, and giant turtles. Fortunately, there is still a bit of magic and mystery, but the mystery is that really unfathomable disturbing kind found in varieties of physical and mental torture. There are champions in these stories too, but their finales are not always a reason for cheering and celebration.

The main purpose of this selection is entertainment. Dahl's verbal boldness will delight you. The passions and interests of his characters will perplex and confuse, but never the way in which they are described – the language is always strong, clear, and steady. Dahl outlines his characters. He knows well the difference between what is enough and what is more than enough to reveal about a character. Often they are not likeable, but even so, they are always intriguing. We are given just the right amount of information and detail, not so much that we can make assumptions about their behaviour, or become sentimental about the characters, but just enough to recognise them, to notice the strangeness in their ordinary lives. Nothing in these stories is beyond your comprehension, but like a good thriller, if you miss the clues or are waylaid by your own imaginings, you will find the story itself "mystifying."

Every one of these stories will cause you to wonder for quite a while after you've finished reading. Sometimes you will be guessing at what exactly happened, why it happened that way or both. Is this the only reason for Dahl's popularity?

This selection demonstrates his ability to write in various

ways on a wide range of subjects and still keep readers of all ages completely enthralled. Of course you may also be horrified or just plain shocked. Here are little people in little worlds appearing huge and monstrous because of what they do and because of the way in which they relate to one another. *The Wish*, the shortest in this collection, is only four pages long, yet offers the same intensity of reading experience as the longest, *Royal Jelly*, because both stories precisely communicate the ambitions and desires of the main characters. Dahl uses various techniques and structures; reportage of events from the standpoint of the detached observer, the child's eye view of adults, the adult's eye view of children, and fairy tales where figures of both good and evil are both limited and stupid.

The interrelationship of human beings and the natural environment is examined in several different ways. Unfortunately the humans don't come out of such an examination looking either too good or too clever – one of Dahl's recurring themes. You will remember that in *A Roald Dahl Selection* this theme is looked at in *The champion of the world* and *The ratcatcher*. It also appears in *James and the giant peach* and several *Revolting rhymes*. The foibles and follies of the adult world dominate *The way up to heaven*, *Poison* and *Royal Jelly* and were it not for the lightness and clarity with which characters in these stories are brought to life, there would be little enjoyment in these stories. Many of Dahl's characters seem unaware of their own capacity for humour. That is part of the puzzle: he writes with humour about people taking themselves seriously, even in the event of a practical joke. No wonder the narrator of *Poison* is called Timber Woods!

The last story in this collection is the first story Dahl wrote. It is interesting to know how *A piece of cake* came to be written, and how Dahl became a writer as a result. You can read the full story in *Lucky Break*, which is in the collection *The wonderful world of Henry Sugar*. Briefly, Dahl didn't plan to meet the famous author C. S. Forester, though he had enjoyed the Hornblower stories. He didn't frequent literary circles, so chances of such a meeting were slight. But one meeting with Forester directed the course of his life and began the flow of stories. Dahl had never intended to become a writer, he had not excelled at essay writing or compositions at school, he had not gone to university. When he finished school, his ambition was to travel and see the world. But he read, he was a reader.

The least miserable days of school had been Saturday when in the morning, guided by an enthusiastic teacher, he learned to read the best of English literature. He learned how to love reading.

Dahl enlisted in the RAF at the outbreak of World War II, and served as a fighter pilot. In 1942, while working as Assistant Air Attaché in Washington, he met C. S. Forester. Dahl had read almost everything Forester had written, those great adventures of danger and travel and the sea. Forester asked Dahl for information about "the most exciting or frightening or dangerous things that happened to you when you were flying fighter planes" so that Forester could write an article for the *Saturday Evening Post*. It was one way Forester had of encouraging Americans in their support of the British during the Second World War. However, as Dahl explains in *Lucky Break*, he had enormous difficulty in putting his experiences into words when talking to Forester. So he offered to provide some written notes. Forester emphasized the need for detail: "Don't worry," he said. "So long as the facts are there, I can write the story. But please," he added, "let me have plenty of detail. That's what counts in our business, tiny little details, like you had a broken shoelace on your left shoe, or a fly settled on the rim of your glass at lunch, or the man you were talking to had a broken front tooth. Try to think back and remember everything."

These examples of detail are worth closer examination. They suggest the atmosphere of what we have come to identify with some of Dahl's stories, the incomplete, the odd, limited damaged characters, the incongruities of unsavoury situations – the fly on the rim of the glass and what do you do? Dahl wrote his first story from his own experiences, describing in vivid detail what it was like to be there in the cockpit, his responses to danger, his conscious and unconscious thoughts and actions, what he remembered exactly and what was only half-remembered. Many writers begin by writing an autobiographical piece, a rigorous exercise in memory and expression from first base – awareness of self. Once that is out of the way it seems easier to create stories about other characters. You may have noticed that English teachers often ask pupils who are new to them to write a short autobiographical piece before going on to other topics for essays. Apart from *A piece of cake, Lucky break*, and *The Mildenhall treasure*, as well as the longer *Boy*, all the rest of Roald Dahl's writing is invention. When you read *Boy* you can frequently spot the ideas which later grew into the gripping and entertaining plots of those Dahl stories now current classics for younger readers. Common to all his stories is the good strong plot, which one way or another tells us something we knew already in a way that surprises. Like all good storytellers he suggests a moral line, without spelling it out, or labouring the point. He invites the reader to define that moral line, so the stories both describe life and question it at the same time.

Roald Dahl concentrates on taking us most frequently into the terrifying territories where people deceive, distrust, torture, and horrify themselves and others. There is not much about loving-kindness and easy friendship in these stories. He tells us about trickery and misunderstanding, the distances between people, the capacity for brutality in men especially, but also in women and children. We are taken into those gloomy recesses of the mind where fear, loathing, cruelty and deceit dominate. The stories do not comfort, they disturb. In our worst imaginings life is without any kindness and understanding. After reading a Roald Dahl short story you are relieved to get out of his imaginary world – it wasn't much to do with joy. But then you are reminded of the existence of truth and warmth and love and humour – it isn't all those little acts of nastiness and their horrifying consequences – not if you remember correctly.

The Swan

The Swan

Ernie had been given a .22 rifle for his birthday. His father, who was already slouching on the sofa watching the telly at nine-thirty on this Saturday morning, said, "Let's see what you can pot, boy. Make yourself useful. Bring us back a rabbit for supper."

"There's rabbits in that big field the other side of the lake," Ernie said. "I seen 'em."

"Then go out and nab one," the father said, picking breakfast from between his front teeth with a split matchstick. "Go out and nab us a rabbit."

"I'll get yer two," Ernie said.

"And on the way back," the father said, "get me a quart bottle of brown ale."

"Gimme the money, then," Ernie said.

The father, without taking his eyes from the TV screen, fished in his pocket for a pound note. "And don't try pinchin' the change like you did last time," he said. "You'll get a thick ear if you do, birthday or no birthday."

"Don't worry," Ernie said.

"And if you want to practise and get your eye in with that gun," the father said, "birds is best. See 'ow many spadgers you can knock down, right?"

"Right," Ernie said. "There's spadgers all the way up the lane in the 'edges. Spadgers is easy."

"If you think spadgers is easy," the father said, "go get yourself a jenny wren. Jenny wrens is 'alf the size of spadgers and they never sit still for one second. Get yourself a jenny wren before you start shootin' yer mouth off about 'ow clever you is."

"Now, Albert," his wife said, looking up from the sink. "That's not nice, shootin' little birds in the nestin' season. I don't mind rabbits, but little birds in the nestin' season is another thing altogether."

"Shut your mouth," the father said. "Nobody's askin' your

opinion. And listen to me, boy," he said to Ernie. "Don't go waving that thing about in the street because you ain't got no licence. Stick it down your trouser-leg till you're out in the country, right?"

"Don't worry," Ernie said. He took the gun and the box of bullets and went out to see what he could kill. He was a big lout of a boy, fifteen years old this birthday. Like his truck-driver father, he had small slitty eyes set very close together near the top of the nose. His mouth was loose, the lips often wet. Brought up in a household where physical violence was an everyday occurrence, he was himself an extremely violent person. Most Saturday afternoons, he and a gang of friends travelled by train or bus to football matches, and if they didn't manage to get into a bloody fight before they returned home, they considered it a wasted day. He took great pleasure in catching small boys after school and twisting their arms behind their backs. Then he would order them to say insulting and filthy things about their own parents.

"Ow! Please don't, Ernie! Please!"

"Say it or I'll twist your arm off!"

They always said it. Then he would give the arm an extra twist and the victim would go off in tears.

Ernie's best friend was called Raymond. He lived four doors away, and he, too, was a big boy for his age. But while Ernie was heavy and loutish, Raymond was tall, slim and muscular.

Outside Raymond's house, Ernie put two fingers in his mouth and gave a long shrill whistle. Raymond came out. "Look what I got for me birthday," Ernie said, showing the gun.

"Cripes!" Raymond said. "We can have some fun with that!"

"Come on, then," Ernie said. "We're goin' up to the big field the other side of the lake to get us a rabbit."

The two boys set off. This was a Saturday morning in May, and the countryside was beautiful around the small village where the boys lived. The chestnut trees were in full flower and the hawthorn was white along the hedges. To reach the big rabbit field, Ernie and Raymond *had* first to walk down a narrow hedgy lane for half a mile. Then they *must* cross the railway line, and go round the big lake where wild ducks and moorhens and coots and ring-ouzels lived. Beyond the lake, over the hill and down the other side, lay the rabbit field. This was all private land belonging to Mr Douglas Highton and the lake itself was a sanctuary for waterfowl.

All the way up the lane, they took turns with the gun, potting at small birds in the hedges. Ernie got a bullfinch and a hedge-sparrow. Raymond got a second bullfinch, a white-throat and a yellowhammer. As each bird was killed, they tied it by the legs to a line of string. Raymond never went anywhere without a big ball of string in his jacket pocket, and a knife. Now they had five little birds dangling on the line of string.

"You know something," Raymond said. "We can eat these."

"Don't talk so daft," Ernie said. "There's not enough meat on one of those to feed a woodlouse."

"There is, too," Raymond said. "The Frenchies eat 'em and so do the Eyeties. Mr Sanders told us about it in class. He said the Frenchies and the Eyeties put up nets and catch 'em by the million and then they eat 'em."

"All right, then," Ernie said. "Let's see 'ow many we can get. Then we'll take 'em 'ome and put 'em in the rabbit stew."

As they progressed up the lane, they shot at every little bird they saw. By the time they got to the railway line, they had fourteen small birds dangling on the line of string.

"Hey!" whispered Ernie, pointing with a long arm. "Look over there!"

There was a group of trees and bushes alongside the railway line, and beside one of the bushes stood a small boy. He was looking up into the branches of an old tree through a pair of binoculars.

"You know who that is?" Raymond whispered back. "It's that little twerp Watson."

"You're right!" Ernie whispered. "It's Watson, the scum of the earth!"

Peter Watson was always the enemy. Ernie and Raymond detested him because he was nearly everything that they were not. He had a small frail body. His face was freckled and he wore spectacles with thick lenses. He was a brilliant pupil, already in the senior class at school although he was only thirteen. He loved music and played the piano well. He was no good at games. He was quiet and polite. His clothes, although patched and darned, were always clean. And his father did not drive a truck or work in a factory. He worked in the bank.

"Let's give the little perisher a fright," Ernie whispered.

The two bigger boys crept up close to the small boy, who didn't see them because he still had binoculars to his eyes.

"*'Ands up!*" shouted Ernie, pointing the gun.

Peter Watson jumped. He lowered the binoculars and stared through his spectacles at the two intruders.

"Go on!" Ernie shouted. "Stick 'em up!"

"I wouldn't point that gun if I were you," Peter Watson said.

"*We're* givin' the orders round 'ere!" Ernie said.

"So stick 'em up," Raymond said, "unless you want a slug in the guts!"

Peter Watson stood quite still, holding the binoculars in front of him with both hands. He looked at Raymond. Then he looked at Ernie. He was not afraid, but he knew better than to play the fool with these two. He had suffered a good deal from their attentions over the years.

"What do you want?" he asked.

"*I want you to stick 'em up!*" Ernie yelled at him. "Can't you understand English?"

Peter Watson didn't move.

"I'll count to five," Ernie said. "And if they're not up by then, you get it in the guts. One . . . Two . . . Three . . ."

Peter Watson raised his arms slowly above his head. It was the only sensible thing to do. Raymond stepped forward and snatched the binoculars from his hands. "What's this?" he snapped. "Who you spyin' on?"

"Nobody."

"Don't lie, Watson. Them things is used for spyin'! I'll bet you was spyin' on us! That's right, ain't it? Confess it!"

"I certainly wasn't spying on you."

"Give 'im a clip over the ear," Ernie said. "Teach 'im not to lie to us."

"I'll do that in a minute," Raymond said. "I'm just workin, meself up."

Peter Watson considered the possibility of trying to escape. All he could do would be to turn and run, and that was pointless. They'd catch him in seconds. And if he shouted for help, there was no one to hear him. All he could do, therefore, was to keep calm and try to talk his way out of the situation.

"Keep them 'ands up!" Ernie barked, waving the barrel of the gun gently from side to side the way he had seen it done by gangsters on the telly. "Go on, laddie, reach!"

9

Peter did as he was told.

"So 'oo was you spyin' on?" Raymond asked. "Out with it!"

"I was watching a green woodpecker," Peter said.

"A what?"

"A male green woodpecker. He was tapping the trunk of that old dead tree, searching for grubs."

"Where is 'ee?" Ernie snapped, raising his gun. "I'll 'ave 'im!"

"No, you won't," Peter said, looking at the string of tiny birds slung over Raymond's shoulder. "He flew off the moment you shouted. Woodpeckers are extremely timid."

"What you watchin' 'im for?" Raymond asked suspiciously. "What's the point? Don't you 'ave nothin' better to do?"

"It's fun watching birds," Peter said. "It's a lot more fun than shooting them."

"Why, you cheeky little bleeder!" Ernie cried. "So you don't like us shootin' birds, eh? Is that what you're sayin'?"

"I think it's absolutely pointless.'

"You don't like anything we do, isn't that right?" Raymond said.

Peter didn't answer.

"Well, let me tell *you* something," Raymond went on. "We don't like anything you do either."

Peter's arm were beginning to ache. He decided to take a risk. Slowly, he lowered them to his sides.

"Up!" yelled Ernie. "Get 'em up!"

"What if I refuse?"

"Blimey! You got a ruddy nerve, ain't you?" Ernie said. "I'm tellin' you for the last time, if you don't stick 'em up I'll pull the trigger!"

"That would be a criminal act," Peter said. "It would be a case for the police."

"And you'd be a case for the 'ospital!" Ernie said.

"Go ahead and shoot," Peter said. "Then they'll send you to Borstal. That's prison."

He saw Ernie hesitate.

"You're really askin' for it, ain't you?" Raymond said.

"I'm simply asking to be left alone," Peter said, "I haven't done you any harm."

"You're a stuck-up little squirt," Ernie said. "That's exactly what you are, a stuck-up little squirt."

Raymond leaned over and whispered something in Ernie's

ear. Ernie listened intently. Then he slapped his thigh and said, "I like it! It's a great idea!"

Ernie placed his gun on the ground and advanced upon the small boy. He grabbed him and threw him to the ground. Raymond took the roll of string from his pocket and cut off a length of it. Together, they forced the boy's arms in front of him and tied his wrists together tight.

"Now the legs," Raymond said. Peter struggled and received a punch in the stomach. That winded him and he lay still. Next, they ties his ankles together with more string. He was now trussed up like a chicken and completely helpless.

Ernie picked up his gun, and then, with his other hand, he grabbed one of Peter's arms. Raymond grabbed the other arm and together they began to drag the boy over the grass towards the railway lines.

Peter kept absolutely quiet. Whatever it was they were up to, talking to them wasn't going to help matters.

They dragged their victim down the embankment and on to the railway lines themselves. Then one took the arms and the other the feet and they lifted him up and laid him down again lengthwise right between two lines.

"You're mad!" Peter said. "You can't do this!"

"'Oo says we can't? This is just a little lesson we're teachin' you not to be cheeky."

"More string," Ernie said.

Raymond produced the ball of string and the two larger boys now proceeded to tie the victim down in such a way that he couldn't wriggle away from between the rails. They did this by looping string around each of his arms and then threading the string under the rails on either side. They did the same with his middle body and his ankles. When they had finished, Peter Watson was strung down helpless and virtually immobile between the rails. The only parts of his body he could move to any extent were his head and feet.

Ernie and Raymond stepped back to survey their handi-work. "We done a nice job," Ernie said.

"There's trains every 'arf 'our on this line," Raymond said. "We ain't gonna 'ave long to wait."

"This is murder!" cried the small boy lying between the rails.

"No it ain't," Raymond told him. "It ain't anything of the sort."

"Let me go! Please let me go! I'll be killed if a train comes along!"

"If you *are* killed, sonny boy," Ernie said, "it'll be your own ruddy fault and I'll tell you why. Because if you lift your 'ead up like you're doin' now, then you've 'ad it, chum! You keep down flat and you might just possibly get away with it. On the other 'and, you might not because I ain't exactly sure 'ow much clearance them trains've got underneath. You 'appen to know, Raymond, 'ow much clearance them trains got underneath?"

"Very little," Raymond said. "They're built ever so close to the ground."

"Might be enough and it might not," Ernie said.

"Let's put it this way," Raymond said. "It'd probably just about be enough for an *ordinary* person like me or you, Ernie. But Mister Watson 'ere I'm not so sure about and I'll tell you why."

"Tell me," Ernie said, egging him on.

"Mister Watson 'ere's got an extra big 'ead, that's why. 'Ee's so flippin' big-'eaded I personally think the bottom bit of the train's goin to scrape 'im whatever 'appens. I'm not saying it's goin' to take 'is 'ead off, mind you. In fact, I'm pretty sure it ain't goin' to do that. But it's goin' to give 'is face a good old scrapin' over. You can be quite sure of that."

"I think you're right," Ernie said.

"It don't do," Raymond said, 'to 'ave a great big swollen 'ead full of brains if you're lyin' on the railway line with a train comin' towards you. That's right, ain't it, Ernie?"

"That's right," Ernie said.

The two bigger boys climbed back up the embankment and sat on the grass behind some bushes. Ernie produced a pack of cigarettes and they both lit up.

Peter Watson, lying helpless between the rails, realized now that they were not going to release him. These were dangerous, crazy boys. They lived for the moment and never considered the consequences. I must try to keep calm and think, Peter told himself. He lay there, quite still, weighing his chances. His chances were good. The highest part of his head was his nose. He estimated the end of his nose was sticking up about four inches above the rails. Was that too much? He wasn't quite sure what clearance these modern diesels had above the ground. It certainly wasn't very much. The back of his head was resting upon loose gravel in between two sleepers. He must try to burrow down a little into the gravel. So he began to wriggle his head from side to side, pushing the gravel away and gradually making for himself a small indentation, a hole in the gravel. In the end, he reckoned he had lowered his head an extra two inches. That would do for the head. But what about the feet? They were sticking up, too. He took care of that by swinging the two tied-together feet over to one side so they lay almost flat.

He waited for the train to come.

Would the driver see him? It was very unlikely for this was the main line, London, Doncaster, York, Newcastle and Scotland, and they used huge long engines in which the driver sat in a cab way back and kept an eye open only for the signals. Along this stretch of the track trains travelled around eighty miles an hour. Peter knew that. He had sat on the bank many times watching them. When he was younger, he used to keep a record of their numbers in a little book, and sometimes the engines had names written on their sides in gold letters.

Either way, he told himself, it was going to be a terrifying business. The noise would be deafening, and the swish of the eighty-mile-an-hour wind wouldn't be much fun either. He wondered for a moment whether there would be any kind of vacuum created underneath the train as it rushed over him, sucking him upward. There might well be. So whatever happened, he must concentrate everything upon pressing his entire body against the ground. Don't go limp. Keep stiff and tense and press down into the ground.

"How're you doin', rat-face!" one of them called out to him from the bushes above. "What's it like waitin' for the execution?"

He decided not to answer. He watched the blue sky above his head where a single cumulus cloud was drifting slowly from left to right. And to keep his mind off the thing that was going to happen soon, he played a game that his father had taught him long ago on a hot summer's day when they were lying on their backs in the grass above the cliffs at Beachy Head. The game was to look for strange faces in the folds and shadows and billows of a cumulus cloud. If you looked hard enough, his father had said, you would always find a face of some sort up there. Peter let his eyes travel slowly over the cloud. In one place, he found a one-eyed man with a beard. In another, there was a long-chinned laughing witch. An aeroplane came across the cloud travelling from east to west. It was a small high-winged monoplane with a red fuselage. An old Piper Club, he thought it was. He watched it until it disappeared.

And then, quite suddenly, he heard a curious little vibrating sound coming from the rails on either side of him. It was very soft, this sound, scarcely audible, a tiny little humming, thrumming whisper that seemed to be coming along the rails from far away.

That's a train, he told himself.

The vibrating along the rails grew louder, then louder still. He raised his head and looked down the long and absolutely straight railway line that stretched away for a mile or more into the distance. It was then that he saw the train. At first it was only a speck, a faraway black dot, but in those few seconds that he kept his head raised, the dot grew bigger and bigger, and it began to take shape, and soon it was no longer a dot but the big, square, blunt front-end of a diesel express. Peter dropped his head and pressed it down hard into the small hole he had dug for it in the gravel. He swung his feet over to one side. He shut his eyes tight and tried to sink his body into the ground.

The train came over him like an explosion. It was as though a gun had gone off in his head. And with the explosion came a tearing, screaming wind that was like a hurricane blowing down his nostrils and into his lungs. The noise was shattering. The wind choked him. He felt as if he were being eaten alive and swallowed up in the belly of a screaming murderous monster.

And then it was over. The train had gone. Peter opened his eyes and saw the blue sky and the big white cloud still drifting overhead. It was all over now and he had done it. He had survived.

"It missed 'im," said a voice.

"What a pity," said another voice.

He glanced sideways and saw the two large louts standing over him.

"Cut 'im loose," Ernie said.

Raymond cut the strings binding him to the rails on either side.

"Undo 'is feet so 'ee can walk, but keep 'is 'ands tied," Ernie said.

Raymond cut the strings around his ankles.

"Get up," Ernie said.

Peter got to his feet.

"You're still a prisoner, matey,' Ernie said.

"What about them rabbits?" Raymond asked. "I thought we was goin' to try for a few rabbits?"

"Plenty of time for that," Ernie answered. "I just thought we'd push the little bleeder into the lake on the way."

"Good," Raymond said. "Cool 'im down."

"You've had your fun," Peter Watson said. "Why don't you let me go now?"

"Because you're a prisoner," Ernie said. "And you ain't just no ordinary prisoner neither. You're a spy. And you know what 'appens to spies when they get caught, don't you? They get put up against the wall and shot."

Peter didn't say any more after that. There was no point at all in provoking those two. The less he said to them and the less he resisted them, the more chance he would have of escaping injury. He had no doubt whatsoever that in their present mood they were capable of doing him quite serious bodily harm. He knew for a fact that Ernie had once broken little Wally Simpson's arm after school and Wally's parents had gone to the police. He had also heard Raymond boasting about what he called "putting the boot in" at the football matches they went to. This, he understood, meant kicking someone in the face or body when he was lying on the ground. They were hooligans, these two, and from what Peter read in his father's newspaper nearly every day, they were not by any means on their own. It seemed the whole country was full of hooligans. They wrecked the interiors of trains, they fought pitched battles in the streets with knives and bicycle chains and metal clubs, they attacked pedestrians, especially other young boys walking alone, and they smashed up roadside cafés. Ernie and Raymond, though perhaps not quite yet fully qualified hooligans, were most definitely on their way.

Therefore, Peter told himself, he must continue to be passive. Do not insult them. Do not aggravate them in any way. And above all, do not try to take them on physically. Then, hopefully, in the end, they might become bored with this nasty little game and go off to shoot rabbits.

The two larger boys had each taken hold of one of Peter's arms and they were marching him across the next field towards the lake. The prisoner's wrists were still tied together in front of him. Ernie carried the gun in his spare hand. Raymond carried the binoculars he had taken from Peter. They came to the lake.

The lake was beautiful on this golden May morning. It was a long and fairly narrow lake with tall willow trees growing here and there along its banks. In the middle, the water was clear and clean, but nearer to the land there was a forest of reeds and bulrushes.

Ernie and Raymond marched their prisoner to the edge of the lake and there they stopped.

"Now then," Ernie said. "What I suggest is this. You take 'is arms and I take 'is legs and we'll swing the little perisher one two three as far out as we can into them nice muddy reeds. 'Ow's that?"

"I like it," Raymond said. "And leave 'is 'ands tied together, right?"

"Right," Ernie said. "'Ow's that with you, snot-nose?"

"If that's what you're going to do, I can't very well stop you," Peter said, trying to keep his voice cool and calm.

"Just you try and stop us," Ernie said, grinning, "and then see what 'appens to you."

"One last question," Peter said. "Did you ever take on somebody your own size?"

The moment he said it, he knew he had made a mistake. He saw the flush coming to Ernie's cheeks and there was a dangerous little spark dancing in his small black eyes.

Luckily, at that very moment, Raymond saved the situation. "Hey! Lookit that bird swimmin' in the reeds over there!" he shouted, pointing. "Let's 'ave 'im!"

It was a mallard drake, with a curvy spoon-shaped yellow beak and a head of emerald green with a white ring round its neck. "Now those you really *can* eat," Raymond went on. "It's a wild duck."

"I'll 'ave 'im!" Ernie cried. He let go of the prisoner's arm and lifted the gun to his shoulder.

"This is a bird sanctuary," Peter said.

"A what?" Ernie asked, lowering the gun.

"Nobody shoots birds here. It's strictly forbidden."

"'Oo says it's forbidden?"

"The owner, Mr Douglas Highton."

"You must be joking," Ernie said and he raised the gun

again. He fired. The duck crumpled in the water.

"Go get 'im," Ernie said to Peter. "Cut 'is 'ands free, Raymond, 'cause then'ee can be our flippin' gun-dog and fetch the birds after we shoot 'em.''

Raymond took out his knife and cut the string binding the small boy's wrists.

"Go on!" Ernie snapped. "Go get 'im!"

The killing of the beautiful duck had disturbed Peter very much. "I refuse," he said.

Ernie hit him across the face hard with his open hand. Peter didn't fall down, but a small trickle of blood began running out of one nostril.

"You dirty little perisher!" Ernie said. "You just try refusin' me one more time and I'm goin' to make you a promise. And the promise is like this. You refuse me just one more time and I'm goin' to knock out every single one of them shiny white front teeth of yours, top and bottom. You understand that?''

Peter said nothing.

"Answer me!" Ernie barked. "Do you understand that?"

"Yes," Peter said quietly. "I understand."

"Get on with it, then!" Ernie shouted.

Peter walked down the bank, into the muddy water, through the reeds, and picked up the duck. He brought it back and Raymond took it from him and tied string around its legs.

"Now we got a retriever dog with us, let's see if we can't get us a few more of them ducks,' Ernie said. He strolled along the bank, gun in hand, searching the reeds. Suddenly he stopped. He crouched. He put a finger to his lips and said, "Sshh!"

Raymond went over to join him. Peter stood a few yards away, his trousers covered in mud up to the knees.

"Lookit in there!" Ernie whispered, pointing into a dense patch of bulrushes. "D'you see what I see?"

"Holy cats!" cried Raymond. "What a beauty!"

Peter, peering from a little further away into the rushes, saw at once what they were looking at. It was a swan, a magnificent white swan sitting serenely upon her nest. The nest itself was a huge pile of reeds and rushes that rose up about two feet above the waterline, and upon the top of all this the swan was sitting like a great white lady of the lake. Her head was turned towards the boys on the bank, alert and watchful.

"'Ow about *that*?" Ernie said. "That's better'n ducks, ain't it?"

"You think you can get 'er?" Raymond said.

"Of course I can get 'er. I'll drill a 'ole right through 'er noggin!"

Peter felt a wild rage beginning to build up inside him. He walked up to the two bigger boys. "I wouldn't shoot that swan if I were you," he said, trying to keep his voice clam. "Swans are the most protected birds in England."

"And what's that got to do with it?" Ernie asked him sneering.

"And I'll tell you something else," Peter went on, throwing all caution away. "Nobody shoots a bird sitting on its nest. Absolutely nobody! She may even have cygnets[1] under her! You just can't do it!"

"'Oo says we can't?" Raymond asked, sneering. "Mister bleedin' snotty-nose Peter Watson, is that the one 'oo says it?"

"The whole country says it," Peter answered. "The law says it and the police say it and *everyone* says it!"

"I don't say it!" Ernie said, raising his gun.

"Don't!" screamed Peter. "Please don't!"

Crack! The gun went off. The bullet hit the swan right in the middle of her elegant head and the long white neck collapsed on to the side of the nest.

"Got 'er!' cried Ernie.

"Hot shot!" shouted Raymond.

Ernie turned to Peter who was standing small and white-faced and absolutely rigid. "Now go get 'er," he ordered.

Once again, Peter didn't move.

Ernie came up close to the smaller boy and bent down and stuck his face right up to Peter's. "I'm tellin' you for the last time," he said, soft and dangerous. "Go get 'er!"

Tears were running down Peter's face as he went slowly down the bank and entered the water. He waded out to the dead swan and picked it up tenderly with both hands. Underneath it were two tiny cygnets, their bodies covered with yellow down. They were huddling together in the centre of the nest.

"Any eggs?" Ernie shouted from the bank.

"No," Peter answered. "Nothing." There was a chance, he

---

[1]   baby swans

18

felt, that when the male swan returned, it would continue to feed the young ones on its own if they were left in the nest. He certainly did not want to leave them to the tender mercies of Ernie and Raymond.

Peter carried the dead swan back to the edge of the lake. He placed it on the ground. The he stood up and faced the two others. His eyes, still wet with tears, where blazing with fury. "That was a filthy thing to do!" he shouted. "It was a stupid pointless act of vandalism! You're a couple of ignorant idiots! It's you who ought to be dead instead of the swan! You're not fit to be alive!"

He stood there, as tall as he could stand, splendid in his fury, facing the two taller boys and not caring any longer what they did to him.

Ernie didn't hit him this time. He seemed just a tiny bit taken aback at first by this outburst, but he quickly recovered. And now his loose lips formed themselves into a sly, wet smirk and his small close-together eyes began to glint in a most malicious[1] manner. "So you like swans, is that right?" he asked softly.

"I like swans and I hate you!" Peter cried.

"And am I right in thinkin'," Ernie went on, still smirking, "am I absolutely right in thinkin' that you wished this old swan down 'ere were alive instead of dead?"

"That's a stupid question!" Peter shouted.

"'Ee needs a clip over the ear-'ole," Raymond said.

"Wait," Ernie said. "I'm doin' this exercise." He turned back to Peter. "So if I could make this swan come alive and go flyin' round the sky all over again, then you'd be 'appy. Right?"

"That's another stupid question!" Peter cried out. "Who d'you think you are?"

"I'll tell you 'oo I am," Ernie said. "I'm a magic man, that's 'oo I am. And just to make you 'appy and contented, I am about to do a magic trick that'll make this dead swan come alive and go flyin' all over the sky once again."

"Rubbish!" Peter said. "I'm going." He turned and started to walk away.

"Grab 'im!" Ernie said.

Raymond grabbed him.

---

[1] wicked, spiteful

"Leave me alone!" Peter cried out.

Raymond slapped him on the cheek, hard. "Now, now," he said. "Don't fight with auntie, not unless you want to get 'urt."

"Gimme your knife," Ernie said, holding out his hand. Raymond gave him his knife.

Ernie knelt down beside the dead swan and stretched out one of its enormous wings. "Watch this," he said.

"What's the big idea?" Raymond asked.

"Wait and see," Ernie said. And now, using the knife, he proceeded to sever the great white wing from the swan's body. There is a joint in the bone where the wing meets the side of the bird, and Ernie located this and slid the knife into the joint and cut through the tendon. The knife was very sharp and it cut well, and soon the wing came away all in one piece.

Ernie turned the swan over and severed the other wing.

"String," he said, holding out his hand to Raymond.

Raymond, who was grasping Peter by the arm, was watching fascinated. "Where'd you learn 'ow to butcher up a bird like that?" he asked.

"With chickens," Ernie said. "We used to nick chickens from up at Stevens Farms and cut 'em up into chicken parts and flog 'em to a shop in Aylesbury. Gimme the string."

Raymond gave him the ball of string. Ernie cut off six pieces, each about a yard long.

There are a series of strong bones running along the top edge of a swan's wing, and Ernie took one of the wings and started tying one end of the bits of string all the way along the top edge of the great wing. When he had done this, he lifted the wing with the six string-ends dangling from it and said to Peter, "Stick out your arms."

"You're absolutely mad!" the smaller boy shouted. "You're demented!"

"Make 'im stick it out," Ernie said to Raymond.

Raymond held up a clenched fist in front of Peter's face and dabbed it gently against his nose. "You see this," he said. "Well I'm goin' to smash you right in the kisser with it unless you do exactly as you're told, see? Now, stick out your arm, there's a good little boy."

Peter felt his resistance collapsing. He couldn't hold out against these people any longer. For a few seconds, he stared at Ernie. Ernie with the tiny close-together black eyes gave the impression he would be capable of doing just about anything if he got really angry. Ernie, Peter felt at that moment, might quite easily kill a person if he were to lose his temper. Ernie, the dangerous backward child, was playing games now and it would be very unwise to spoil his fun. Peter held out an arm.

Ernie then proceeded to tie the six string ends one by one to Peter's arm, and when he had finished, the white wing of the swan was securely attached along the entire length of the arm itself.

"Ow's that, eh?" Ernie said, stepping back and surveying his work.

"Now the other one," Raymond said, catching on to what Ernie was doing. "You can't expect 'im to go flyin' round the sky with only one wing, can you?"

"Second wing comin' up," Ernie said. He knelt down again and tied six more lengths of string to the top bones of the second wing. Then he stood up again. "Let's 'ave the other arm," he said. Peter, feeling sick and ridiculous, held out his other arm. Ernie strapped the wing tightly along the length of it.

"Now!" Ernie cried, clapping his hands and dancing a little jig on the grass. "Now we got ourselves a real live swan all over again! Didn't I tell you I was a magic man? Didn't I tell you I was goin' to do a magic trick and make this dead swan come alive and go flyin' all over the sky? Didn't I tell you that?"

Peter stood there in the sunshine beside the lake on this beautiful May morning, the enormous, limp and slightly bloodied wings dangling grotesquely at his sides. "Have you finished?" he said.

"Swans don't talk," Ernie said, "Keep your flippin' beak shut! And save your energy, laddie, because you're goin' to need all the strength and energy you got when it comes to flyin' round in the sky." Ernie picked up his gun from the ground, then he grabbed Peter by the back of the neck with his free hand and said, "March!"

They marched along the bank of the lake until they came to a tall and graceful willow tree. There they halted. The tree was a weeping willow, and the long branches hung down from a great height and almost touched the surface of the lake.

"And now the magic swan is goin' to show us a bit of magic flyin'," Ernie announced. "So what you're goin' to do, Mister Swan, is to climb up to the very top of this tree, and when you

21

get there you're goin' to spread out your wings like a clever little swannee-swan-swan and you're goin' to take off!"

"Fantastic!" cried Raymond. "Terrific! I like it very much!"

"So do I," Ernie said. "Because now we're goin' to find out just exactly 'ow clever this clever little swannee-swan-swan really is. 'Ee's terribly clever at school, we all know that, and 'ee's top of the class and everything else that's lovely, but let's see just exactly 'ow clever 'ee is when 'ee's at the top of the tree! Right, Mister Swan?" He gave Peter a push towards the tree.

How much further could this madness go? Peter wondered. He was beginning to feel a little mad himself, as though nothing was real any more and none of it was actually happening. But the thought of being high up in the tree and out of reach of these hooligans at last was something that appealed to him greatly. When he was up there, he could stay up there. He doubted very much if they would bother to come up after him. And even if they did, he could surely climb away from them along a thin limb that would not take the weight of two people.

The tree was a fairly easy one to climb, with several low branches to give him a start up. He began climbing. The huge white wings dangling from his arms kept getting in the way, but it didn't matter. What mattered now to Peter was that every inch upward was another inch away from his tormentors below. He had never been a great one for tree-climbing and he wasn't especially good at it, but nothing in the world was going to stop him from getting to the top of this one. And once he was there, he thought it unlikely they would even be able to see him because of the leaves.

"Higher!" shouted Ernie's voice. "Keep goin'!"

Peter kept going, and eventually he arrived at a point where it was impossible to go higher. His feet were now standing on a branch that was about as thick as a person's wrist, and this particular branch reached far out over the lake and then curved gracefully downward. All the branches above him were very thin and whippy, but the one he was holding on to with his hands was quite strong enough for the purpose. He stood there, resting after the climb. He looked down for the first time. He was very high up, at least fifty feet. But he couldn't see the two boys. They were no longer standing at the base of the tree. Was it possible they had gone away at last?

"All right, Mister Swan!" came the dreaded voice of Ernie. "Now listen carefully!"

The two of them had walked some distance away from the tree to a point where they had a clear view of the small boy at the top. Looking down at them now, Peter realized how very sparse and slender the leaves of a willow tree were. They gave him almost no cover at all.

"Listen carefully, Mister Swan!" the voice was shouting. "Start walking out along that branch you're standin' on! Keep goin' till you're right over the nice muddy water! Then you take off!"

Peter didn't move. He was fifty feet above them now and they weren't ever going to reach him again. From down below, there was a long silence. It lasted maybe half a minute. He kept his eyes on the two distant figures in the field. They were standing quite still, looking up at him.

"All right then, Mister Swan!" came Ernie's voice again. "I'm gonna count to ten, right? And if you ain't spread them wings and flown away by then, I'm gonna shoot you down instead with this little gun! And that'll make two swans I've knocked off today instead of one! So here we go, Mister Swan! One! . . . Two! . . . Three! . . . Four! . . . Five! . . . Six! . . ."

Peter remained still. Nothing would make him move from now on.

"Seven! . . . Eight! . . . Nine! . . . Ten!"

Peter saw the gun coming up to the shoulder. It was pointing straight at him. Then he heard the *crack* of the rifle and the *zip* of the bullet as it whistled past his head. It was a frightening thing. But he still didn't move. He could see Ernie loading the gun with another bullet.

"Last chance!" yelled Ernie. "The next one's gonna get you!"

Peter stayed put. He waited. He watched the boy who was standing among the buttercups in the meadow far below with the other boy beside him. The gun came up once again to the shoulder.

This time he heard the *crack* at the same instant the bullet hit him in the thigh. There was no pain, but the force of it was devastating. It was as though someone had whacked him on the leg with a sledgehammer, and it knocked both feet off the branch he was standing on. He scrabbled with his hands to hang on. The small branch he was holding on to bent over and split.

Some people, when they have taken too much and have been driven beyond the point of endurance, simply crumble and give up. There are others, though they are not many, who will for some reason always be unconquerable. You meet them in time of war and also in time of peace. They have an indomitable spirit and nothing, neither pain nor torture nor threat of death, will cause them to give up.

Little Peter Watson was one of these. And as he fought and scrabbled to prevent himself from falling out of the top of that tree, it came to him suddenly that he was going to win. He looked up and he saw a light shining over the waters of the lake that was of such brilliance and beauty he was unable to look away from it. The light was beckoning him, drawing him on, and he dived towards the light and spread his wings.

Three different people reported seeing a great white swan circling over the village that morning, a school-teacher called Emily Mead, a man who was replacing some tiles on the roof of the chemist's shop whose name was William Eyles, and a boy called John Underwood who was flying his model aeroplane in a nearby field.

And that morning, Mrs Watson, who was washing up some dishes in her kitchen sink, happened to glance up through the window at the exact moment when something huge and white came flopping down on to the lawn in her back garden. She rushed outside. She went down on her knees beside the small crumpled figure of her only son. "Oh, my darling!" she cried, near to hysterics and hardly believing what she saw. "My darling boy! What happened to you?"

"My leg hurts," Peter said, opening his eyes. Then he fainted.

"It's bleeding!" she cried and she picked him up and carried him inside. Quickly she phoned for the doctor and the ambulance. And while she was waiting for help to come, she fetched a pair of scissors and began cutting the string that held the two great wings of the swan to her son's arms.

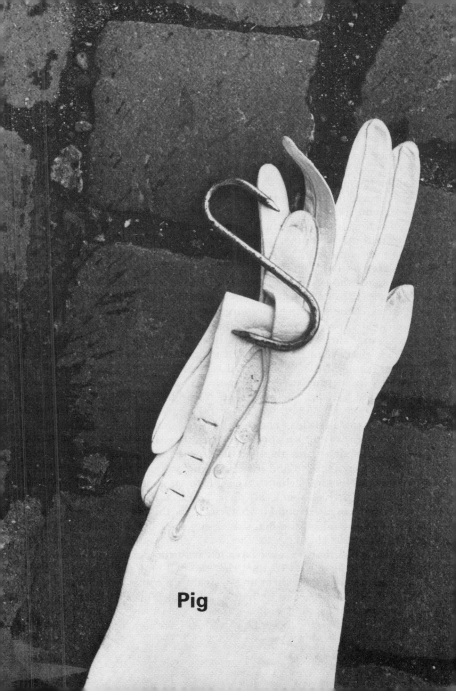

Pig

Pig

1

Once upon a time, in the City of New York, a beautiful baby boy was born into this world, and the joyful parents named him Lexington.

No sooner had the mother returned home from the hospital carrying Lexington in her arms than she said to her husband, "Darling, now you must take me out to a most marvellous restaurant for dinner so that we can celebrate the arrival of our son and heir."

Her husband embraced her tenderly and told her that any woman who could produce such a beautiful child as Lexington deserved to go absolutely anywhere she wanted. But was she strong enough yet, he inquired, to start running around the city late at night?

"No," she said, she wasn't. But what the hell.

So that evening both dressed themselves up in fancy clothes, and leaving little Lexington in care of a trained infant's nurse who was costing them twenty dollars a day and was Scottish into the bargain, they went out to the finest and most expensive restaurant in town. There they each ate a giant lobster and drank a bottle of champagne between them, and after that, they went on to a nightclub, where they drank another bottle of champagne and then sat holding hands for several hours while they recalled and discussed and admired each individual physical feature of their lovely newborn son.

They arrived back at their house on the East Side of Manhattan at around two o'clock in the morning and the husband paid off the taxi driver and then began feeling in his pockets for the key to the front door. After a while, he announced that he must have left it in the pocket of his other suit, and he suggested they ring the bell and get the nurse to come down and let them in. An infant's nurse at twenty dollars a day must expect to be hauled out of bed occasionally in the night, the husband said.

So he rang the bell. They waited. Nothing happened. He

26

rang it again, long and loud. They waited another minute. Then they both stepped back on to the street and shouted the nurse's name (McPottle) up at the nursery windows on the third floor, but there was still no response. The house was dark and silent. The wife began to grow apprehensive.[1] Her baby was imprisoned in this place, she told herself. Alone with McPottle. And who was McPottle? They had known her for two days, that was all, and she had a thin mouth, a small disapproving eye, and a starchy bosom, and quite clearly she was in the habit of sleeping too soundly for safety. If she couldn't hear the front-door bell, then how on earth did she expect to hear a baby crying? Why, this very second the poor thing might be swallowing its tongue or suffocating on its pillow.

"He doesn't use a pillow," the husband said. "You are not to worry. But I'll get you in if that's what you want." He was feeling rather superb after all the champagne, and now he bent down and undid the laces of one of his black patent-leather shoes, and took it off. Then, holding it by the toe, he flung it hard and straight through the dining-room window on the ground floor.

"There you are," he said, grinning. "We'll deduct it from McPottle's wages."

He stepped forward and very carefully put a hand through the hole in the glass and released the catch. Then he raised the window.

"I shall lift you in first, little mother," he said, and he took his wife around the waist and lifted her off the ground. This brought her big red mouth up level with his own, and very close, so he started kissing her. He knew from experience that women like very much to be kissed in this position, with their bodies held tight and their legs dangling in the air, so he went on doing it for quite a long time, and she wiggled her feet, and made loud gulping noises down in her throat. Finally, the husband turned her round and began easing her gently through the open window into the dining-room. At this point, a police patrol car came nosing silently along the street towards them. It stopped about thirty yards away, and three cops of Irish extraction[2] leaped out of the car and started

[1] uneasy
[2] coming from Ireland, of Irish descent

running in the direction of the husband and wife, brandishing revolvers.

"Stick 'em up!" the cops shouted. "Stick 'em up!" But it was impossible for the husband to obey this order without letting go of his wife, and had he done this she would either have fallen to the ground or would have been left dangling half in and half out of the house, which is a terribly uncomfortable position for a woman; so he continued gallantly to push her upward and inward through the window. The cops, all of whom had received medals before for killing robbers, opened fire immediately, and although they were still running, and although the wife in particular was presenting them with a very small target indeed, they succeeded in scoring several direct hits on each body – sufficient anyway to prove fatal in both cases.

Thus, when he was no more than twelve days old, little Lexington became an orphan.

2

The news of this killing, for which the three policemen subsequently received citations,[1] was eagerly conveyed to all relatives of the deceased couple by newspaper reporters, and the next morning the closest of these relatives, as well as a couple of undertakers, three lawyers, and a priest, climbed into taxis and set out for the house with the broken window. They assembled in the living-room, men and women both, and they sat around in a circle on the sofas and armchairs, smoking cigarettes and sipping sherry and debating what on earth should be done now with the baby upstairs, the orphan Lexington.

It soon became apparent that none of the relatives was particularly keen to assume responsibility for the child, and the discussions and arguments continued all through the day. Everybody declared an enormous, almost an irresistible desire to look after him, and would have done so with the greatest of pleasure were it not for the fact that their apartment was too small, or that they already had one baby and couldn't possibly afford another, or that they wouldn't know what to

---

[1] recognition of achievement

do with the poor little thing when they went abroad in the summer, or that they were getting on in years, which surely would be most unfair to the boy when he grew up, and so on and so forth. They all knew, of course, that the father had been heavily in debt for a long time and that the house was mortgaged and that consequently there would be no money at all to go with the child.

They were still arguing like mad at six in the evening when suddenly, in the middle of it all, an old aunt of the deceased father (her name was *Glosspan*) swept in from Virginia, and without even removing her hat and coat, not even pausing to sit down, ignoring all offers of a martini, a whisky, a sherry, she announced firmly to the assembled relatives that she herself intended to take sole charge of the infant boy from then on. What was more, she said, she would assume full financial responsibility on all counts, including education, and everyone else could go back home where they belonged and give their consciences a rest. So saying, she trotted upstairs to the nursery and snatched Lexington from his cradle and swept out of the house with the baby clutched tightly in her arms, while the relatives simply sat and stared and smiled and looked relieved, and McPottle the nurse stood stiff with disapproval at the head of the stairs, her lips compressed, her arms folded across her starchy bosom.

And thus it was that the infant Lexington, when he was thirteen days old, left the City of New York and travelled southward to live with his Great Aunt Glosspan in the State of Virginia.

3

Aunt Glosspan was nearly seventy when she became guardian to Lexington, but to look at her you would never have guessed it for one minute. She was as sprightly as a woman half her age, with a small, wrinkled, but still quite beautiful face and two lovely brown eyes that sparkled at you in the nicest way. She was also a spinster, though you would never have guessed that either, for there was nothing spinsterish about Aunt Glosspan. She was never bitter or gloomy or irritable; she didn't have a moustache; and she wasn't in the least bit jealous of other people, which in itself is something you can seldom say about either a spinster or a virgin lady, although of course it is not known for certain whether Aunt Glosspan qualified on both counts.

But she was an eccentric old woman, there was no doubt about that. For the past thirty years she had lived a strange isolated life all by herself in a tiny cottage high up on the slopes of the Blue Ridge Mountains, several miles from the nearest village. She had five acres of pasture,[1] a plot for growing vegetables, a flower garden, three cows, a dozen hens, and a fine cockerel.

And now she had little Lexington as well.

She was a strict vegetarian and regarded the consumption of animal flesh as not only unhealthy and disgusting, but horribly cruel. She lived upon lovely clean foods like milk, butter, eggs, cheese, vegetables, nuts, herbs, and fruit, and she rejoiced in the conviction that no living creature would be slaughtered on her account, not even a shrimp. Once, when a brown hen of hers passed away in the prime of life from being eggbound, Aunt Glosspan was so distressed that she nearly gave up egg-eating altogether.

She knew not the first thing about babies, but that didn't worry her in the least. At the railway station in New York, while waiting for the train that would take her and Lexington back to Virginia, she bought six feeding-bottles, two dozen diapers, a box of safety pins, a carton of milk for the journey, and a small paper-covered book called *The Care of Infants*. What more could anyone want? And when the train got going, she fed the baby some milk, changed its nappies after a fashion, and laid it down on the seat to sleep. Then she read *The Care of Infants* from cover to cover.

"There is no problem here," she said, throwing the book out of the window. "No problem at all."

And curiously enough there wasn't. Back home in the cottage everything went just as smoothly as could be. Little Lexington drank his milk and belched and yelled and slept exactly as a good baby should, and Aunt Glosspan glowed with joy whenever she looked at him and showered him with kisses all day long.

---

[1] fields for animals to graze, feed

4

By the time he was six years old, young Lexington had grown into the most beautiful boy with long golden hair and deep blue eyes the colour of cornflowers. He was bright and cheerful, and already he was learning to help his old aunt in all sorts of different ways around the property, collecting the eggs from the chicken house, turning the handle of the butter churn, digging up potatoes in the vegetable garden, and searching for wild herbs on the side of the mountain. Soon, Aunt Glosspan told herself, she would have to start thinking about his education.

But she couldn't bear the thought of sending him away to school. She loved him so much now that it would kill her to be parted from him for any length of time. There was, of course, that village school down in the valley, but it was a dreadful-looking place, and if she sent him there she just knew they would start forcing him to eat meat the very first day he arrived.

"You know what, my darling?" she said to him one day when he was sitting on a stool in the kitchen watching her make cheese. "I don't really see why I shouldn't give you your lessons myself."

The boy looked up at her with his large blue eyes, and gave her a lovely trusting smile. "That would be nice," he said.

"And the very first thing I should do would be to teach you how to cook."

"I think I would like that, Aunt Glosspan."

"Whether you like it or not, you're going to have to learn some time," she said. "Vegetarians like us don't have nearly so many foods to choose from as ordinary people, and therefore they must learn to be doubly expert with what they have."

"Aunt Glosspan," the boy said, "what *do* ordinary people eat that we don't?"

"Animals," she answered, tossing her head in disgust.

"You mean *live* animals?"

"No," she said. "Dead ones."

The boy considered this for a moment.

"You mean when they die they *eat* them instead of *burying* them?"

"They don't wait for them to die, my pet. They kill them."

"How do they kill them, Aunt Glosspan?"

"They usually slit their throats with a knife."

"But what *kind* of animals?"

"Cows and pigs mostly, and sheep."

"Cows!" the boy cried. "You mean like Daisy and Snow-drop and Lily?"

"Exactly, my dear."

"But *how* do they eat them, Aunt Glosspan?"

"They cut them up into bits and they cook the bits. They like it best when it's all red and bloody and sticking to the bones. They love to eat lumps of cow's flesh with the blood oozing out of it."

"Pigs too?"

"They adore pigs."

"Lumps of bloody pig's meat," the boy said. "Imagine that. What else do they eat, Aunt Glosspan?"

"Chickens."

"Chickens!"

"Millions of them."

"Feathers and all?"

"No, dear, not the feathers. Now run along outside and get Aunt Glosspan a bunch of chives, will you, my darling?"

Shortly after that, the lessons began. They covered five subjects, reading, writing, geography, arithmetic, and cooking, but the latter was by far the most popular with both teacher and pupil. In fact, it very soon became apparent that young Lexington possessed a truly remarkable talent in this direction. He was a born cook. He was dextrous[1] and quick. He could handle his pans like a juggler. He could slice a single potato into twenty paper-thin slivers in less time than it took his aunt to peel it. His palate was exquisitely sensitive, and he could taste a pot of strong onion soup and immediately detect the presence of a single tiny leaf of sage. In so young a boy, all this was a bit bewildering to Aunt Glosspan, and to tell the truth she didn't quite know what to make of it. But she was proud as proud could be, all the same, and predicted a brilliant future for the child.

"What a mercy it is," she said, "that I have such a wonderful little fellow to look after me in my dotage."[2] And a couple of years later, she retired from the kitchen for good,

[1] clever with his hands
[2] childishness of old age

leaving Lexington in sole charge of all household cooking. The boy was now ten years old, and Aunt Glosspan was nearly eighty.

5

With the kitchen to himself, Lexington straight away began experimenting with dishes of his own invention. The old favourites no longer interested him. He had a violent urge to create. There were hundreds of fresh ideas in his head. "I will begin," he said, "by devising a chestnut soufflé." He made it and served it up for supper that very night. It was terrific. "You are a genius!" Aunt Glosspan cried, leaping up from her chair and kissing him on both cheeks. "You will make history!"

From then on, hardly a day went by without some new delectable creation being set upon the table. There was Brazilnut soup, hominy cutlets, vegetable ragout, dandelion omelette, cream-cheese fritters, stuffed-cabbage surprise, stewed foggage,[1] shallots *à la bonne femme*, beetroot mousse piquant,[2] prunes Stroganoff, Dutch rarebit, turnips on horseback, flaming spruce-needle tarts, and many many other beautiful compositions. Never before in her life, Aunt Glosspan declared, had she tasted such food as this; and in the morning, long before lunch was due, she would go out on to the porch and sit there in her rocking-chair, speculating about the coming meal, licking her chops, sniffing the aromas that came wafting out through the kitchen window.

"What's that you're making in there today, boy?" she would call out.

"Try to guess, Aunt Glosspan."

"Smells like a bit of salsify fritters to me," she would say, sniffing vigorously.

Then out he would come, this ten-year-old child, a little grin of triumph on his face, and in his hands a big steaming pot of the most heavenly stew made entirely of parsnips and lovage.[3]

"You know what you ought to do," his aunt said to him,

---

[1] grass that grows after hay is cut
[2] nice sharp flavour
[3] salad plant

gobbling the stew. "You ought to set yourself down this very minute with paper and pencil and write a cooking-book."

He looked at her across the table, chewing his parsnips slowly.

"Why not?" she cried. "I've taught you how to write and I've taught you how to cook and now all you've got to do is put the two things together. You write a cooking-book, my darling, and it'll make you famous the whole world over."

"All right," he said. "I will."

And that very day, Lexington began writing the first page of that monumental work which was to occupy him for the rest of his life. He called it *Eat Good and Healthy*.

6

Seven years later, by the time he was seventeen, he had recorded over nine thousand different recipes, all of them original, all of them delicious.

But now, suddenly, his labours were interrupted by the tragic death of Aunt Glosspan. She was afflicted in the night by a violent seizure, and Lexington, who had rushed into her bedroom to see what all the noise was about, found her lying on her bed yelling and cussing and twisting herself up into all manner of complicated knots. Indeed, she was a terrible sight to behold, and the agitated youth danced around her in his pyjamas, wringing his hands, and wondering what on earth he should do. Finally, in an effort to cool her down, he fetched a bucket of water from the pond in the cow field and tipped it over her head, but this only intensified the paroxysms,[1] and the old lady expired within the hour.

"This is really too bad," the poor boy said, pinching her several times to make sure that she was dead. "And how sudden! How quick and sudden! Why only a few hours ago she seemed in the very best of spirits. She even took three large helpings of my most recent creation, devilled mushroom burgers, and told me how succulent it was."

After weeping bitterly for several minutes, for he had loved his aunt very much, he pulled himself together and carried her outside and buried her behind the cowshed.

[1] fit of acute pain

The next day, while tidying up her belongings, he came across an envelope that was addressed to him in Aunt Glosspan's hand-writing. He opened it and drew out two fifty-dollar bills and a letter.

Darling boy [the letter said,] I know that you have never yet been down the mountain since you were thirteen days old, but as soon as I die you must put on a pair of shoes and a clean shirt and walk down to the village and find the doctor. Ask the doctor to give you a death certificate to prove that I am dead. Then take this certificate to my lawyer, a man called Mr Samuel Zuckermann, who lives in New York City and who has a copy of my will. Mr Zuckermann will arrange everything. The cash in this envelope is to pay the doctor for the certificate and to cover the cost of your journey to New York. Mr Zuckermann will give you more money when you get there, and it is my earnest wish that you use it to further your researches into culinary and vegetarian matters, and that you continue to work upon that great book of yours until you are satisfied that it is complete in every way. Your loving aunt – Glosspan

Lexington, who had always done everything his aunt told him, pocketed the money, put on a pair of shoes and a clean shirt, and went down the mountain to the village where the doctor lived.

"Old Glosspan?" the doctor said. "My God, is *she* dead?"

"Certainly she's dead," the youth answered. "If you will come back home with me now I'll dig her up and you can see for yourself."

"How deep did you bury her?" the doctor asked.

"Six or seven feet down, I should think."

"And how long ago?"

"Oh, about eight hours."

"Then she's dead," the doctor announced. "Here's the certificate."

7

Our hero now sets out for the City of New York to find Mr Samuel Zuckermann. He travelled on foot, and he slept under hedges, and he lived on berries and wild herbs, and it took him sixteen days to reach the metropolis.

"What a fabulous place this is!" he cried as he stood at the corner of Fifty-seventh Street and Fifth Avenue, staring around him. "There are no cows or chickens anywhere, and none of the women looks in the least like Aunt Glosspan."

As for Mr Samuel Zuckermann, he looked like nothing that Lexington had ever seen before.

He was a small spongy man with livid jowls[1] and a huge magenta[2] nose, and when he smiled, bits of gold flashed at you marvellously from lots of different places inside his mouth. In his luxurious office, he shook Lexington warmly by the hand and congratulated him upon his aunt's death.

"I suppose you knew that your dearly beloved guardian was a woman of considerable wealth?" he said.

"You mean the cows and chickens?"

"I mean half a million bucks," Mr Zuckermann said.

"How much?"

"Half a million dollars, my boy. And she's left it all to you." Mr Zuckermann leaned back in his chair and clasped his hands over his spongy paunch. At the same time, he began secretly working his right forefinger in through his waistcoat and under his shirt so as to scratch the skin around the circumference of his navel – a favourite exercise of his, and one that gave him a peculiar pleasure. "Of course, I shall have to deduct fifty per cent for my services," he said, "but that still leaves you with two hundred and fifty grand."

"I am rich!" Lexington cried. "This is wonderful! How soon can I have the money?"

"Well," Mr Zuckermann said, "luckily for you, I happen to be on rather cordial terms with the tax authorities around here, and I am confident that I shall be able to persuade them to waive all death duties and back taxes."

"How kind you are," murmured Lexington.

"I should naturally have to give somebody a small honorarium."[3]

"Whatever you say, Mr Zuckermann."

"I think a hundred thousand would be sufficient."

"Good gracious, isn't that rather excessive?"

---

[1] discoloured loose flesh around jaw
[2] reddish purple
[3] voluntary fee

"Never undertip a tax inspector or a policeman," Mr Zuckermann said. "Remember that."

"But how much does it leave for me?" the youth asked meekly.

"One hundred and fifty thousand. But then you've got the funeral expenses to pay out of that."

"*Funeral* expenses?"

"You've got to pay the funeral parlour. Surely you know that?"

"But I buried her myself, Mr Zuckermann, behind the cowshed."

"I don't doubt it," the lawyer said. "So what?"

"I never used a funeral parlour."

"Listen," Mr Zuckermann said patiently. "You may not know it, but there is a law in this State which says that no beneficiary under a will may receive a single penny of his inheritance until the funeral parlour has been paid in full."

"You mean that's a *law*?"

"Certainly it's a law, and a very good one it is, too. The funeral parlour is one of our great national institutions. It must be protected at all costs."

Mr Zuckermann himself, together with a group of public-spirited doctors, controlled a corporation that owned a chain of nine lavish funeral parlours in the city, not to mention a casket factory in Brooklyn and a postgraduate school for embalmers in Washington Heights. The celebration of death was therefore a deeply religious affair in Mr Zuckermann's eyes. In fact, the whole business affected him profoundly, almost as profoundly, one might say, as the birth of Christ affected the shopkeeper.

"You had no right to go out and bury your aunt like that," he said. "None at all."

"I'm very sorry, Mr Zuckermann."

"Why, its downright subversive."[1]

"I'll do whatever you say, Mr Zuckermann. All I want to know is how much I'm going to get in the end, when everything's paid."

There was a pause. Mr Zuckerman sighed and frowned and continued secretly to run the tip of his finger around the rim of his navel.

---

[1] intending to overthrow

"Shall we say fifteen thousand?" he suggested, flashing a big gold smile. "That's a nice round figure."

"Can I take it with me this afternoon?"

"I don't see why not."

So Mr Zuckermann summoned his chief cashier and told him to give Lexington fifteen thousand dollars out of the petty cash, and to obtain a receipt. The youth, who by this time was delighted to be getting anything at all, accepted the money gratefully and stowed it away in his knapsack. Then he shook Mr Zuckermann warmly by the hand, thanked him for all his help, and went out of the office.

"The whole world is before me!" our hero cried as he emerged into the street. "I now have fifteen thousand dollars to see me through until my book is published. And after that, of course, I shall have a great deal more." He stood on the pavement, wondering which way to go. He turned left and began strolling slowly down the street, staring at the sights of the city.

"What a revolting smell," he said, sniffing the air. "I can't stand this." His delicate olfactory[1] nerves, tuned to receive only the most delicious kitchen aromas, were being tortured by the stench of the diesel-oil fumes pouring out of the backs of the buses.

"I must get out of this place before my nose is ruined altogether," he said. "But first, I've simply got to have something to eat. I'm starving." The poor boy had had nothing but berries and wild herbs for the past two weeks, and now his stomach was yearning for solid food. I'd like a nice hominy[2] cutlet, he told himself. Or maybe a few juicy salsify[3] fritters.

He crossed the street and entered a small restaurant. The place was hot inside, and dark and silent. There was a strong smell of cooking-fat and cabbage water. The only other customer was a man with a brown hat on his head, crouching intently over his food, who did not look up as Lexington came in.

Our hero seated himself at a corner table and hung his knapsack on the back of his chair. This, he told himself, is going to be most interesting. In all my seventeen years I have

[1]   concerned with smelling
[2]   crushed, boiled maize
[3]   root vegetable

tasted only the cooking of two people, Aunt Glosspan and myself – unless one counts Nurse McPottle, who must have heated my bottle a few times when I was an infant. But I am now about to sample the art of a new chef altogether, and perhaps, if I am lucky, I may pick up a couple of useful ideas for my book.

A waiter approached out of the shadows at the back, and stood beside the table.

"How do you do," Lexington said. "I should like a large hominy cutlet please. Do it twenty-five seconds each side, in a very hot skillet with sour cream, and sprinkle a pinch of lovage on it before serving – unless of course your chef knows of a more original method, in which case I should be delighted to try it."

The waiter laid his head over to one side and looked carefully at his customer. "You want the roast pork and cabbage?" he asked. "That's all we got left."

"Roast what and cabbage?"

The waiter took a soiled handkerchief from his trouser pocket and shook it open with a violent flourish, as though he were cracking a whip. Then he blew his nose loud and wet.

"You want it or don't you?" he said, wiping his nostrils.

"I haven't the foggiest idea what it is," Lexington replied, "but I should love to try it. You see, I am writing a cooking-book and . . ."

"One pork and cabbage!" the waiter shouted, and somewhere in the back of the restaurant, far away in the darkness, a voice answered him.

The waiter disappeared. Lexington reached into his knapsack for his personal knife and fork. These were a present from Aunt Glosspan, given him when he was six years old, made of solid silver, and he had never eaten with any other instruments since. While waiting for the food to arrive, he polished them lovingly with a piece of soft muslin.

Soon the waiter returned carrying a plate on which there lay a thick greyish-white slab of something hot. Lexington leaned forward anxiously to smell it as it was put down before him. His nostrils were wide open now to receive the scent, quivering and sniffing.

"But this is absolute heaven!" he exclaimed. "What an aroma! It's tremendous!"

The waiter stepped back a pace, watching his customer carefully.

"Never in my life have I smelled anything as rich and wonderful as this!" our hero cried, seizing his knife and fork. "What on earth is it made of?"

The man in the brown hat looked around and stared, then returned to his eating. The waiter was backing away towards the kitchen.

Lexington cut off a small piece of the meat, impaled it on his silver fork, and carried it up to his nose so as to smell it again. Then he popped it into his mouth and began to chew it slowly, his eyes half closed, his body tense.

"This is fantastic!" he cried. "It is a brand-new flavour! Oh Glosspan, my beloved Aunt, how I wish you were with me now so you could taste this remarkable dish! Waiter! Come here at once! I want you!"

The astonished waiter was now watching from the other end of the room, and he seemed reluctant to move any closer.

"If you will come and talk to me I will give you a present," Lexington said, waving a hundred-dollar bill. "Please come over here and talk to me."

The waiter sidled cautiously back to the table, snatched away the money, and held it up close to his face, peering at it from all angles. Then he slipped it quickly into his pocket.

"What can I do for you, my friend?" he asked.

"Look," Lexington said. "If you will tell me what this delicious dish is made of, and exactly how it is prepared, I will give you another hundred."

"I already told you," the man said. "It's pork."

"And what exactly is pork?"

"You never had roast pork before?" the waiter asked, staring.

"For heaven's sake, man, tell me what it is and stop keeping me in suspense like this."

"It's pig," the waiter said. "You just bung it in the oven."

"*Pig!*"

"All pork is pig. Didn't you know that?"

"You mean *this* is *pig's* meat?"

"I guarantee it."

"But . . . but . . . that's impossible," the youth stammered. "Aunt Glosspan, who knew more about food than anyone else in the world, said that meat of any kind was disgusting, revolting, horrible, foul, nauseating, and beastly. And yet this piece that I have here on my plate is without doubt the most delicious thing that I have ever tasted. Now how on earth do you explain that? Aunt Glosspan certainly wouldn't have told me it was revolting if it wasn't."

"Maybe your aunt didn't know how to cook it," the waiter said.

"Is that possible?"

"You're damned right it is. Especially with pork. Pork has to be very well done or you can't eat it."

"Eureka!" Lexington cried. "I'll bet that's exactly what happened! She did it wrong!" He handed the man another hundred-dollar bill. "Lead me to the kitchen," he said. "Introduce me to the genius who prepared this meat."

Lexington was at once taken into the kitchen, and there he met the cook who was an elderly man with a rash on one side of his neck.

"This will cost you another hundred," the waiter said.

Lexington was only too glad to oblige, but this time he gave the money to the cook. "Now listen to me," he said. "I have to admit that I am really rather confused by what the waiter has just been telling me. Are you quite positive that the delectable dish which I have just been eating was prepared from pig's flesh?"

The cook raised his right hand and began scratching the rash on his neck.

"Well," he said, looking at the waiter and giving him a sly wink, "all I can tell you is that I *think* it was pig's meat."

"You mean you're not sure?"

"One can't ever be sure."

"Then what else could it have been?"

"Well," the cook said, speaking very slowly and still staring at the waiter. "There's just a chance, you see, that it might have been a piece of human stuff."

"You mean a man?"

"Yes."

"Good heavens."

"Or a woman. It could have been either. They both taste the same."

"Well – now you really do surprise me," the youth declared.

"One lives and learns."

"Indeed one does."

"As a matter of fact, we've been getting an awful lot of it just lately from the butcher's in place of pork," the cook declared.

"Have you really?"

"The trouble is, it's almost impossible to tell which is which. They're both very good."

"The piece I had just now was simply superb."

"I'm glad you liked it," the cook said. "But to be quite honest, I think that was a bit of pig. In fact, I'm almost sure it was."

"You are?"

"Yes, I am."

"In that case, we shall have to assume that you are right," Lexington said. "So now will you please tell me – and here is another hundred dollars for your trouble – will you please tell me precisely how you prepared it?"

The cook, after pocketing the money, launched out upon a colourful description of how to roast a loin of pork, while the youth, not wanting to miss a single word of so great a recipe, sat down at the kitchen table and recorded every detail in his notebook.

"Is that all?" he asked when the cook had finished.

"That's all."

"But there must be more to it than that, surely?"

"You got to get a good piece of meat to start off with," the cook said. "That's half the battle. It's got to be a good hog and it's got to be butchered right, otherwise it'll turn out lousy which ever way you cook it."

"Show me how," Lexington said. "Butcher me one now so I can learn."

"We don't butcher pigs in the kitchen," the cook said. "That lot you just ate came from a packing-house over in the Bronx."

"Then give me the address!"

The cook gave him the address, and our hero, after thanking them both many times for all their kindnesses, rushed outside and leapt into a taxi and headed for the Bronx.

8

The packing-house was a big four-story brick building, and the air around it smelled sweet and heavy, like musk. At the main entrance gates, there was a large notice which said VISITORS WELCOME AT ANY TIME, and thus encouraged, Lexington walked through the gates and entered a cobbled yard which surrounded the building itself. He then followed a series of signposts (THIS WAY FOR THE GUIDED TOURS), and came eventually to a small corrugated-iron shed set well apart from the main building (VISITORS' WAITING-ROOM). After knocking politely on the the door, he went in.

There were six other people ahead of him in the waiting-room. There was a fat mother with her two little boys aged about nine and eleven. There was a bright-eyed young couple who looked as though they might be on their honeymoon. And there was a pale woman with long white gloves, who sat very upright, looking straight ahead, with her hands folded on her lap. Nobody spoke. Lexington wondered whether they were all writing cooking-books, like himself, but when he put this question to them aloud, he got no answer. The grown-ups merely smiled mysteriously to themselves and shook their heads, and the two children stared at him as though they were seeing a lunatic.

Soon, the door opened and a man with a merry pink face popped his head into the room and said, "Next, please." The mother and the two boys got up and went out.

About ten minutes later, the same man returned. "Next, please," he said again, and the honeymoon couple jumped up and followed him outside.

Two new visitors came in and sat down – a middle-aged husband and a middle-aged wife, the wife carrying a wicker shopping-basket containing groceries.

"Next, please," said the guide, and the woman with the long white gloves got up and left.

Several more people came in and took their places on the stiff-backed wooden chairs.

Soon the guide returned for the third time, and now it was Lexington's turn to go outside.

"Follow me, please," the guide said, leading the youth across the yard towards the main building.

"How exciting this is!" Lexington cried, hopping from one foot to the other. "I only wish that my dear Aunt Glosspan could be with me now to see what I am going to see."

"I myself only do the preliminaries," the guide said. "Then I shall hand you over to someone else."

"Anything you say," cried the ecstatic youth.

First they visited a large penned-in area at the back of the building where several hundred pigs were wandering around. "Here's where they start," the guide said. "And over there's where they go in."

"Where?"

"Right there." The guide pointed to a long wooden shed that stood against the outside wall of the factory. "We call it the shackling-pen. This way, please."

Three men wearing long rubber boots were driving a dozen pigs into the shackling-pen just as Lexington and the guide approached, so they all went in together.

"Now," the guide said, "watch how they shackle them."

Inside, the shed was simply a bare wooden room with no roof, but there was a steel cable with hooks on it that kept moving slowly along the length of one wall, parallel with the ground, about three feet up. When it reached the end of the shed, this cable suddenly changed direction and climbed vertically upward through the open roof towards the top floor of the main building.

The twelve pigs were huddled together at the far end of the pen, standing quietly, looking apprehensive. One of the men in rubber boots pulled a length of metal chain down from the wall and advanced upon the nearest animal, approaching it from the rear. Then he bent down and quickly looped one end of the chain around one of the animal's hind legs. The other end he attached to a hook on the moving cable as it went by. The cable kept moving. The chain tightened. The pig's leg was pulled up and back, and then the pig itself began to be dragged backwards. But it didn't fall down. It was rather a nimble pig, and somehow it managed to keep its balance on three legs, hopping from foot to foot and struggling against the pull of the chain, but going back and back all the time until at the end of the pen where the cable changed direction and went vertically upward, the creature was suddenly jerked off its feet and borne aloft. Shrill protests filled the air.

"Truly a fascinating process," Lexington said. "But what was the funny cracking noise it made as it went up?"

"Probably the leg," the guide answered. "Either that or the pelvis."

44

"But doesn't that matter?"

"Why should it matter?" the guide asked. "You don't eat the bones."

The rubber-booted men were busy shackling the rest of the pigs, and one after another they were hooked to the moving cable and hoisted up through the roof, protesting loudly as they went.

"There's a good deal more to this recipe than just picking herbs," Lexington said. "Aunt Glosspan would never have made it."

At this point, while Lexington was gazing skyward at the last pit to go up, a man in rubber boots approached him quietly from behind and looped one end of a chain around the youth's own ankle, hooking the other end to the moving belt. The next moment, before he had time to realize what was happening, our hero was jerked off his feet and dragged backwards along the concrete floor of the shackling-pen.

"Stop!" he cried. "Hold everything! My leg is caught!"

But nobody seemed to hear him, and five seconds later, the unhappy young man was jerked off the floor and hoisted vertically upward through the open roof of the pen, dangling upside down by one ankle, and wriggling like a fish.

"Help!" he shouted. "Help! There's been a frightful mistake! Stop the engines! Let me down!"

The guide removed a cigar from his mouth and looked up serenely at the rapidly ascending youth, but he said nothing. The men in rubber boots were already on their way out to collect the next batch of pigs.

"Oh, save me!" our hero cried. "Let me down! Please let me down!" But he was now approaching the top floor of the building where the moving belt curled over like a snake and entered a large hole in the wall, a kind of doorway without a door; and there, on the threshold, waiting to greet him, clothed in a dark-stained yellow rubber apron, and looking for all the world like Saint Peter at the Gates of Heaven, the sticker stood.

Lexington saw him only from upside down, and very briefly at that, but even so he noticed at once the expression of absolute peace and benevolence on the man's face, the cheerful twinkle in the eyes, the little wistful smile, the dimples in his cheeks – and all this gave him hope.

"Hi there," the sticker said, smiling.

"Quick! Save me!" our hero cried.

"With pleasure," the sticker said, and taking Lexington gently by one ear with his left hand, he raised his right hand and deftly slit open the boy's jugular vein with a knife.

The belt moved on. Lexington went with it. Everything was still upside down and the blood was pouring out of his throat and getting into his eyes, but he could still see after a fashion, and he had a blurred impression of being in an enormously long room, and at the far end of the room there was a great smoking cauldron of water, and there were dark figures, half hidden in the steam, dancing around the edge of it, brandishing long poles. The conveyor-belt seemed to be travelling right over the top of the cauldron, and the pigs seemed to be dropping down one by one into the boiling water, and one of the pigs seemed to be wearing long white gloves on its front feet.

Suddenly our hero started to feel very sleepy, but it wasn't until his good strong heart had pumped the last drop of blood from his body that he passed on out of this, the best of all possible worlds, into the next.

The Boy Who Talked With Animals

The Boy Who Talked with Animals

Not so long ago, I decided to spend a few days in the West Indies. I was to go there for a short holiday. Friends had told me it was marvellous. I would laze around all day, they said, sunning myself on the silver beaches and swimming in the warm green sea.

I chose Jamaica, and flew direct from London to Kingston. The drive from Kingston airport to my hotel on the north shore took two hours. The island was full of mountains and the mountains were covered all over with dark tangled forests. The big Jamaican who drove the taxi told me that up in those forests lived whole communities of diabolical[1] people who still practised voodoo and witch-doctory and other magic rites.

"Don't ever go up into those mountain forests," he said, rolling his eyes. "There's things happening up there that'd make your hair turn white in a minute!"

"What sort of things?" I asked him.

"It's better you don't ask," he said. "It don't pay even to talk about it." And that was all he would say on the subject.

My hotel lay upon the edge of a pearly beach, and the setting was even more beautiful than I had imagined. But the moment I walked in through those big open front doors, I began to feel uneasy. There was no reason for this. I couldn't see anything wrong. But the feeling was there and I couldn't shake it off. There was something weird and sinister about the place. Despite all the loveliness and the luxury, there was a whiff of danger that hung and drifted in the air like a poisonous gas.

And I wasn't sure it was just the hotel. The whole island, the mountains and the forests, the black rocks along the coastline and the trees cascading with brilliant scarlet flowers, all these and many other things made me feel uncomfortable in

---

[1]   dreadful, appalling

my skin. There was something malignant[1] crouching underneath the surface of this island. I could sense it in my bones.

My room in the hotel had a little balcony, and from there I could step straight down on to the beach. There were tall coconut palms growing all around, and every so often an enormous green nut the size of a football would fall out of the sky and drop with a thud on the sand. It was considered foolish to linger underneath a coconut palm because if one of those things landed on your head, it would smash your skull.

The Jamaican girl who came in to tidy my room told me that a wealthy American called Mr Wasserman had met his end in precisely this manner only two months before.

"You're joking," I said to her.

"Not joking!" she cried. "No *suh*! I sees it happening with my very own eyes!"

"But wasn't there a terrific fuss about it?" I asked.

"They hush it up," she answered darkly. "The hotel folks hush it up and so do the newspaper folks because things like that are very bad for the tourist business."

"And you say you actually saw it happen?"

"I actually saw it happen," she said. "Mr Wasserman, he's standing right under that very tree over there on the beach. He's got his camera out and he's pointing it at the sunset. It's a red sunset that evening, and very pretty. Then all at once, down comes a big green nut right smack on to the top of his bald head. *Wham!* And that," she added with a touch of relish, "is the very last sunset Mr Wasserman ever did see."

"You mean it killed him instantly?"

"I don't know about *instantly*," she said. "I remember the next thing that happens is the camera falls out of his hands on to the sand. Then his arms drop down to his sides and hang there. Then he starts swaying. He sways backwards and forwards several times ever so gentle, and I'm standing there watching him, and I says to myself the poor man's gone all dizzy and maybe he's going to faint any moment. Then very very slowly he keels right over and down he goes."

"Was he dead?"

"Dead as a doornail," she said.

"Good heavens."

[1] harmful

"That's right," she said. "It never pays to be standing under a coconut palm when there's a breeze blowing."

"Thank you," I said. "I'll remember that."

On the evening of my second day, I was sitting on my little balcony with a book on my lap and a tall glass of rum punch in my hand. I wasn't reading the book. I was watching a small green lizard stalking another small green lizard on the balcony floor about six feet away. The stalking lizard was coming up on the other one from behind, moving forward very slowly and very cautiously, and when he came within reach, he flicked out a long tongue and touched the other one's tail. The other one jumped round, and the two of them faced each other, motionless, glued to the floor, crouching, staring and very tense. Then suddenly, they started doing a funny little hopping dance together. They hopped up in the air. They hopped backwards. They hopped forwards. They hopped sideways. They circled one another like two boxers, hopping and prancing and dancing all the time. It was a queer thing to watch, and I guessed it was some sort of a courtship ritual they were going through. I kept very still, waiting to see what was going to happen next.

But I never saw what happened next because at that moment I became aware of a great commotion[1] on the beach below. I glanced over and saw a crowd of people clustering around something at the water's edge. There was a narrow canoe-type fisherman's boat pulled up on the sand nearby, and all I could think of was that the fisherman had come in with a lot of fish and that the crowd was looking at it.

A haul of fish is something that has always fascinated me. I put my book aside and stood up. More people were trooping down from the hotel veranda and hurrying over the beach to join the crowd on the edge of the water. The men were wearing those frightful Bermuda shorts that came down to the knees, and their shirts were bilious[2] with pinks and oranges and every other clashing colour you could think of. The women had better taste, and were dressed for the most part in pretty cotton dresses. Nearly everyone carried a drink in one hand.

I picked up my own drink and stepped down from the balcony on to the beach. I made a little detour around the

[1] noisy confusion
[2] sickly

coconut palm under which Mr Wasserman had supposedly
met his end, and strode across the beautiful silvery sand to join
the crowd.

But it wasn't a haul of fish they were staring at. It was a
turtle, an upside-down turtle lying on its back in the sand. But
what a turtle it was! It was a giant, a mammoth. I had not
thought it possible for a turtle to be as enormous as this. How
can I describe its size? Had it been the right way up, I think
a tall man could have sat on its back without his feet touching
the ground. It was perhaps five feet long and four feet across,
with a high domed shell of great beauty.

The fisherman who had caught it had tipped it on to its back
to stop it from getting away. There was also a thick rope tied
around the middle of its shell, and one proud fisherman, slim
and black and naked except for a small loincloth, stood a short
way off holding the end of the rope with both hands.

Upside down it lay, this magnificent creature, with its four
thick flippers waving frantically in the air, and its long wrinkled neck stretching far out of its shell. The flippers had large
sharp claws on them.

"Stand back, ladies and gentlemen, please!" cried the fisherman. "Stand well back! Them claws is *dangerous*, man!
They'll rip your arm clear away from your body!"

The crowd of hotel guests was thrilled and delighted by this
spectacle. A dozen cameras were out and clicking away. Many
of the women were squealing with pleasure clutching on to the
arms of their men, and the men were demonstrating their lack
of fear and their masculinity by making foolish remarks in loud
voices.

"Make yourself a nice pair of horn-rimmed spectacles out
of that shell, hey Al?"

"Darn thing must weigh over a ton!"

"You mean to say it can actually float?"

"Sure it floats. Powerful swimmer, too. Pull a boat easy."

"He's a snapper, is he?"

"That's no snapper. Snapper turtles don't grow as big as
that. But I'll tell you what. He'll snap your hand off quick
enough if you get too close to him."

"Is that true?" one of the women asked the fisherman.
"Would he snap off a person's hand?"

"He would right now," the fisherman said, smiling with
brilliant white teeth. "He won't ever hurt you when he's in the

ocean, but you catch him and pull him ashore and tip him up like this, then man alive, you'd better watch out! He'll snap at anything that comes in reach!"

"I guess I'd get a bit snappish myself," the woman said, "if I was in his situation."

One idiotic man had found a plank of driftwood on the sand, and he was carrying it towards the turtle. It was a fair-sized plank, about five feet long and maybe an inch thick. He started poking one end of it at the turtle's head.

"I wouldn't do that," the fisherman said. "You'll only make him madder than ever."

When the end of the plank touched the turtle's neck, the great head whipped round and the mouth opened wide and *snap*, it took the plank in its mouth and bit through it as if it were made of cheese.

"Wow!" they shouted. "Did you see that! I'm glad it wasn't my arm!"

"Leave him alone," the fisherman said. "It don't help to get him all stirred up."

A paunchy man with wide hips and very short legs came up to the fisherman and said, "Listen, feller. I want that shell. I'll buy it from you." And to his plump wife, he said, "You know what I'm going to do, Mildred? I'm going to take that shell home and have it polished up by an expert. Then I'm going to place it smack in the centre of our living-room! Won't that be something?"

"Fantastic," the plump wife said. "Go ahead and buy it, baby."

"Don't worry," he said. "It's mine already." And to the fisherman, he said, "How much for the shell?"

"I already sold him," the fisherman said. "I sold him shell and all."

"Not so fast, feller," the paunchy man said. "I'll bid you higher. Come on. What'd he offer you?"

"No can do," the fisherman said. "I already sold him."

"Who to?" the paunchy man said.

"To the manager."

"What manager?"

"The manager of the hotel."

"Did you hear that?" shouted another man. "He's sold it to the manager of our hotel! And you know what that means? It means turtle soup, that's what it means!"

"Right you are! And turtle steak! You ever have a turtle steak, Bill?"

"I never have, Jack. But I can't wait."

"A turtle steak's better than a beefsteak if you cook it right. It's more tender and it's got one heck of a flavour."

"Listen," the paunchy man said to the fisherman. "I'm not trying to buy the meat. The manager can have the meat. He can have everything that's inside including the teeth and toenails. All I want is the shell."

"And if I know you, baby," his wife said, beaming at him, "you're going to get the shell."

I stood there listening to the conversation of these human beings. They were discussing the destruction, the consumption and the flavour of a creature who seemed, even when upside down, to be extraordinarily dignified. One thing was certain. He was senior to any of them in age. For probably one hundred and fifty years he had been cruising in the green waters of the West Indies. He was there when George Washington was President of the United States and Napoleon was being clobbered at Waterloo. He would have been a small turtle then, but he was most certainly there.

And now he was here, upside down on the beach, waiting to be sacrificed for soup and steak. He was clearly alarmed by all the noise and the shouting around him. His old wrinkled neck was straining out of its shell, and the great head was twisting this way and that as though searching for someone who would explain the reason for all this ill-treatment.

"How are you going to get him up to the hotel?" the paunchy man asked.

"Drag him up the beach with the rope," the fisherman answered. "The staff'll be coming along soon to take him. It's going to need ten men, all pulling at once."

"Hey, listen!" cried a muscular young man. "Why don't *we* drag him up?" The muscular young man was wearing magenta[1] and pea-green Bermuda shorts and no shirt. He had an exceptionally hairy chest, and the absence of a shirt was obviously a calculated touch. "What say we do a little work for our supper?" he cried, rippling his muscles. "Come on, fellers! Who's for some exercise?"

"Great idea!" they shouted. "Splendid scheme!"

---

[1] reddish purple

The men handed their drinks to the women and rushed to catch hold of the rope. They ranged themselves along it as though for a tug-of-war, and the hairy-chested man appointed himself anchor-man and captain of the team.

"Come on, now, fellers!" he shouted. "When I say *heave*, then all heave at once, you understand?"

The fisherman didn't like this much. "It's better you leave this job for the hotel," he said.

"Rubbish!" shouted hairy-chest. "*Heave*, boys, *heave!*"

They all heaved. The gigantic turtle wobbled on its back and nearly toppled over.

"Don't tip him!" yelled the fisherman. "You're going to tip him over if you do that! And if once he gets back on to his legs again, he'll escape for sure!"

"Cool it, laddie," said hairy-chest in a patronizing voice. "How can he escape? We've got a rope round him, haven't we?"

"The old turtle will drag the whole lot of you away with him if you give him a chance!" cried the fisherman. "He'll drag you out into the ocean, every one of you!"

"*Heave!*" shouted hairy-chest, ignoring the fisherman. "*Heave*, boys, *heave!*"

And now the gigantic turtle began very slowly to slide up the beach towards the hotel, towards the kitchen, towards the place where the big knives were kept. The womenfolk and the older, fatter, less athletic men followed alongside, shouting encouragement.

"*Heave!*" shouted the hairy-chested anchor-man. "Put your backs into it, fellers! You can pull harder than that!"

Suddenly, I heard screams. Everyone heard them. They were screams so high-pitched, so shrill and so urgent they cut right through everything. "No-o-o-o-o!" screamed the scream. "No! No! No! No! No!"

The crowd froze. The tug-of-war men stopped tugging and the onlookers stopped shouting and every single person present turned towards the place where the streams were coming from.

Half walking, half running down the beach from the hotel, I saw three people, a man, a woman and a small boy. They were half running because the boy was pulling the man along. The man had the boy by the wrist, trying to slow him down, but the boy kept pulling. At the same time, he was jumping and twisting and wriggling and trying to free himself from the father's grip. It was the boy who was screaming.

"Don't!" he screamed. "Don't do it! Let him go! Please let him go!"

The woman, his mother, was trying to catch hold of the boy's other arm to help restrain him, but the boy was jumping about so much, she didn't succeed.

"Let him go!" screamed the boy. "It's horrible what you're doing! Please let him go!"

"Stop that, David!" the mother said, still trying to catch his other arm. "Don't be so childish! You're making a perfect fool of yourself."

"Daddy!" the boy screamed. "Daddy! Tell them to let him go!"

"I can't do that, David," the father said. "It isn't any of our business."

The tug-of-war pullers remained motionless, still holding the rope with the gigantic turtle on the end of it. Everyone stood silent and surprised, staring at the boy. They were all a bit off-balance now. They had the slightly hangdog air of people who had been caught doing something that was not entirely honourable.

"Come on now, David," the father said, pulling against the boy. "Let's go back to the hotel and leave these people alone."

"I'm not going back!" the boy shouted. "I don't want to go back! I want them to let it go!"

"Now, David," the mother said.

"Beat it, kid," the hairy-chested man told the boy.

"You're horrible and cruel!" the boy shouted. "All of you are horrible and cruel!" He threw the words high and shrill at the forty or fifty adults standing there on the beach, and nobody, not even the hairy-chested man, answered him this time. "Why don't you put him back in the sea?" the boy shouted. "He hasn't done anything to you! Let him go!"

The father was embarrassed by his son, but he was not ashamed of him. "He's crazy about animals," he said, addressing the crowd. "Back home he's got every kind of animal under the sun. He talks with them."

"He loves them," the mother said.

Several people began shuffling their feet around in the sand. Here and there in the crowd it was possible to sense a slight change of mood, a feeling of uneasiness, a touch even of shame. The boy, who could have been no more than eight or nine years old had stopped struggling with his father now. The father still held him by the wrist, but he was no longer restraining him.

"Go on!" the boy called out. "Let him go! Undo the rope and let him go!" He stood very small and erect, facing the crowd, his eyes shining like two stars and the wind blowing in his hair. He was magnificent.

"There's nothing we can do, David," the father said gently. "Let's go on back."

"No!" the boy cried out, and at that moment he suddenly gave a twist and wrenched his wrist free from the father's grip. He was away like a streak, running across the sand towards the giant upturned turtle.

"David!" the father yelled, starting after him. "Stop! Come back!"

The boy dodged and swerved through the crowd like a player running with the ball, and the only person who sprang forward to intercept[1] him was the fisherman. "Don't you go near that turtle, boy!" he shouted as he made a lunge for the swiftly running figure. But the boy dodged round him and kept going. "He'll bite you to pieces!" yelled the fisherman. "Stop, boy! Stop!"

But it was too late to stop him now, and as he came running straight at the turtle's head, the turtle saw him, and the huge upside-down head turned quickly to face him.

The voice of the boy's mother, the stricken, agonized wail of the mother's voice rose up into the evening sky. "David!" it cried. "*Oh, David!*" And a moment later, the boy was throwing himself on to his knees in the sand and flinging his arms around the wrinkled old neck and hugging the creature to his chest. The boy's cheek was pressing against the turtle's head, and his lips were moving, whispering soft words that nobody else could hear. The turtle became absolutely still. Even the giant flippers stopped waving in the air.

A great sigh, a long soft sigh of relief, went up from the crowd. Many people took a pace or two backward, as though trying perhaps to get a little further away from something that was beyond their understanding. But the father and mother came forward together and stood about ten feet away from their son.

[1] stop

56

"Daddy!" the boy cried out, still caressing the old brown head. "Please do something, Daddy! Please make them let him go!"

"Can I be of any help here?" said a man in a white suit who had just come down from the hotel. This, as everyone knew, was Mr Edwards, the manager. He was a tall, beak-nosed Englishman with a long pink face. "*What* an extraordinary thing!" he said, looking at the boy and the turtle. "He's lucky he hasn't had his head bitten off." And to the boy he said, "You'd better come away from there now, sonny. That thing's dangerous."

"I want them to let him go!" cried the boy, still cradling the head in his arms. "Tell them to let him go!"

"You realize he could be killed any moment," the manager said to the boy's father.

"Leave him alone," the father said.

"Rubbish," the manager said. "Go in and grab him. But be quick. And be careful."

"No," the father said.

"What do you mean, no?" said the manager. "These things are lethal! Don't you understand that?"

"Yes," the father said.

"Then for heaven's sake, man, get him away!" cried the manager. "There's going to be a very nasty accident if you don't."

"Who owns it?" the father said. "Who owns the turtle?"

"We do," the manager said. "The hotel has bought it."

"Then do me a favour," the father said. "Let me buy it from you."

The manager looked at the father, but said nothing.

"You don't know my son," the father said, speaking quietly. "He'll go crazy if it's taken up to the hotel and slaughtered. He'll become hysterical."

"Just pull him away," the manager said. "And be quick about it."

"He loves animals," the father said. "He really loves them. He communicates with them."

The crowd was silent, trying to hear what was being said. Nobody moved away. They stood as though hypnotized.

"If we let it go," the manager said, "they'll only catch it again."

"Perhaps they will," the father said. "But those things can swim."

"I know they can swim," the manager said. "They'll catch him all the same. This is a valuable item, you must realize that. The shell alone is worth a lot of money."

"I don't care about the cost," the father said. "Don't worry about that. I want to buy it."

The boy was still kneeling in the sand beside the turtle, caressing its head.

The manager took a handkerchief from his breast pocket and started wiping his fingers. He was not keen to let the turtle go. He probably had the dinner menu already planned. On the other hand, he didn't want another gruesome accident on his private beach this season. Mr Wasserman and the coconut, he told himself, had been quite enough for one year, thank you very much.

The father said, "I would deem it a great personal favour, Mr Edwards, if you would let me buy it. And I promise you won't regret it. I'll make quite sure of that."

The manager's eyebrows went up just a fraction of an inch. He had got the point. He was being offered a bribe. That was a different matter. For a few seconds he went on wiping his hands with the handkerchief. Then he shrugged his shoulders and said, "Well, I suppose if it will make your boy feel any better . . ."

"Thank you," the father said.

"Oh, thank you!" the mother cried. "Thank you so very much!"

"Willy," the manager said, beckoning to the fisherman.

The fisherman came forward. He looked thoroughly confused. "I never seen anything like this before in my whole life," he said. "This old turtle was the fiercest I ever caught! He fought like a devil when we brought him in! It took all six of us to land him! That boy's crazy!"

"Yes, I know," the manager said. "But now I want you to let him go."

"Let him go!" the fisherman cried, aghast. "You mustn't ever let this one go, Mr Edwards! He's broke the record! He's the biggest turtle ever been caught on this island! Easy the biggest! And what about our money?"

"You'll get your money."

"I got the other five to pay off as well," the fisherman said, pointing down the beach.

About a hundred yards down, on the water's edge, five

black-skinned almost naked men were standing beside a second boat. "All six of us are in on this, equal shares," the fisherman went on. "I can't let him go till we got the money."

"I guarantee you'll get it," the manager said. "Isn't that good enough for you?"

"I'll underwrite[1] that guarantee," the father of the boy said, stepping forward. "And there'll be an extra bonus for all six of the fishermen just as long as you let him go at once. I mean immediately, this instant."

The fisherman looked at the father. Then he looked at the manager. "Okay," he said. "If that's the way you want it."

"There's one condition," the father said. "Before you get your money, you must promise you won't go straight out and try to catch him again. Not this evening, anyway. Is that understood?"

"Sure," the fisherman said. "That's a deal." He turned and ran down the beach, calling to the other five fishermen. He shouted something to them that we couldn't hear, and in a minute or two, all six of them came back together. Five of them were carrying long thick wooden poles.

The boy was still kneeling beside the turtle's head. "David," the father said to him gently. "It's all right now, David. They're going to let him go."

The boy looked round, but he didn't take his arms from around the turtle's neck, and he didn't get up. "When?" he asked.

"Now," the father said. "Right now. So you'd better come away."

"You promise?" the boy said.

"Yes, David, I promise."

The boy withdrew his arms. He got his feet. He stepped back a few paces.

"Stand back everyone!" shouted the fisherman called Willy. "Stand right back everyone, please!"

The crowd moved a few yards up the beach. The tug-of-war men let go the rope and moved back with the others.

Willy got down on his hands and knees and crept very cautiously up to one side of the turtle. Then he began untying the knot in the rope. He kept well out of the range of the big flippers as he did this.

[1] put my name to

When the knot was untied, Willy crawled back. Then the five other fishermen stepped forward with their poles. The poles were about seven feet long and immensely thick. They wedged them underneath the shell of the turtle and began to rock the great creature from side to side on its shell. The shell had a high dome and was well shaped for rocking.

"Up and down!" sang the fishermen as they rocked away. "Up and down! Up and down! Up and down!" The old turtle became thoroughly upset, and who could blame it? The big flippers lashed the air frantically, and the head kept shooting in and out of the shell.

"Roll him over!" sang the fishermen. "Up and over! Roll him over! One more time and over he goes!"

The turtle tilted high up on to its side and crashed down in the sand the right way up.

But it didn't walk away at once. The huge brown head came out and peered cautiously[1] around.

"Go, turtle, go!" the small boy called out. "Go back to the sea!"

The two hooded black eyes of the turtle peered up at the boy. The eyes were bright and lively, full of the wisdom of great age. The boy looked back at the turtle, and this time when he spoke, his voice was soft and intimate. "Good-bye, old man," he said. "Go far away this time." The black eyes remained resting on the boy for a few seconds more. Nobody moved. Then, with great dignity, the massive beast turned away and began waddling towards the edge of the ocean. He didn't hurry. He moved sedately[2] over the sandy beach, the big shell rocking gently from side to side as he went.

The crowd watched in silence.

He entered the water.

He kept going.

Soon he was swimming. He was in his element now. He swam gracefully and very fast, with the head held high. The sea was calm, and he made little waves that fanned out behind him on both sides, like the waves of a boat. It was several minutes before we lost sight of him, and by then he was half-way to the horizon.

[1]   carefully
[2]   calmly

The guests began wandering back towards the hotel. They were curiously subdued.[1] There was no joking or bantering[2] now, no laughing. Something had happened. Something strange had come fluttering across the beach.

I walked back to my small balcony and sat down with a cigarette. I had an uneasy feeling that this was not the end of the affair.

The next morning at eight o'clock, the Jamaican girl, the one who had told me about Mr Wasserman and the coconut, brought a glass of orange juice to my room.

"Big *big* fuss in the hotel this morning," she said as she placed the glass on the table and drew back the curtains. "Everyone flying about all over the place like they was crazy."

"Why? What's happened?"

"That little boy in number twelve, he's vanished. He disappeared in the night."

"You mean the turtle boy?"

"That's him," she said. "His parents is raising the roof and the manager's going mad."

"How long's he been missing?"

"About two hours ago his father found his bed empty. But he could've gone any time in the night I reckon."

"Yes," I said. "He could."

"Everybody in the hotel searching high and low," she said. "And a police car just arrived."

"Maybe he just got up early and went for a climb on the rocks," I said.

Her large dark haunted-looking eyes rested a moment on my face, then travelled away. "I do not think so," she said, and out she went.

I slipped on some clothes and hurried down to the beach. On the beach itself, two native policemen in khaki uniforms were standing with Mr Edwards, the manager. Mr Edwards was doing the talking. The policemen were listening patiently. In the distance, at both ends of the beach, I could see small groups of people, hotel servants as well as hotel guests, spreading out and heading for the rocks. The morning was beautiful. The sky was smoke blue, faintly glazed with yellow.

---

[1]   under control
[2]   speaking playfully

The sun was up and making diamonds all over the smooth sea. And Mr Edwards was talking loudly to the two native policemen, and waving his arms.

I wanted to help. What should I do? Which way should I go? It would be pointless simply to follow the others. So I just kept walking towards Mr Edwards.

About then, I saw the fishing-boat. The long wooden canoe with a single mast and a flapping brown sail was still some way out to sea, but it was heading for the beach. The two natives aboard, one at either end, were paddling hard. They were paddling very hard. The paddles rose and fell at such a terrific speed they might have been in a race. I stopped and watched them. Why the great rush to reach the shore? Quite obviously they had something to tell. I kept my eyes on the boat. Over to my left, I could hear Mr Edwards saying to the two policemen, "It is perfectly ridiculous. I can't have people disappearing just like that from the hotel. You'd better find him fast, you understand me? He's either wandered off somewhere and got lost or he's been kidnapped. Either way, it's the responsibility of the police . . ."

The fishing-boat skimmed over the sea and came gliding up on to the sand at the water's edge. Both men dropped their paddles and jumped out. They started running up the beach. I recognized the one in front as Willy. When he caught sight of the manager and the two policemen, he made straight for them.

"Hey, Mr Edwards!" Willy called out. "We just seen a crazy thing!"

The manager stiffened and jerked back his neck. The two policemen remained impassive.[1] They were used to excitable people. They met them every day.

Willy stopped in front of the group, his chest heaving in and out with heavy breathing. The other fisherman was close behind him. They were both naked except for a tiny loincloth, their black skins shining with sweat.

"We been paddling full speed for a long way," Willy said, excusing his out-of-breathness. "We thought we ought to come back and tell it as quick as we can.

"Tell what?" the manager said. "What did you see?"

"It was crazy, man! Absolutely crazy!"

[1] showed no feeling

"Get on with it, Willy, for heaven's sake."

"You won't believe it," Willy said. "There ain't nobody going to believe it. Isn't that right, Tom?"

"That's right," the other fisherman said, nodding vigorously.[1] "If Willy here hadn't been with me to prove it, I wouldn't have believed it myself!"

"Believed what?" Mr Edwards said. "Just tell us what you saw."

"We'd gone off early," Willy said, "about four o'clock this morning, and we must've been a couple of miles out before it got light enough to see anything properly. Suddenly, as the sun comes up, we see right ahead of us, not more'n fifty yards away, we see something we couldn't believe not even with our eyes . . ."

"What?" snapped Mr Edwards. "For heaven's sake get on!"

"We sees that old monster turtle swimming away out there, the one on the beach yesterday, and we sees the boy sitting high up on the turtle's back and riding him over the sea like a horse!"

"You gotta believe it!" the other fisherman cried. "I sees it too, so you gotta believe it!"

Mr Edwards looked at the two policemen. The two policemen looked at the fishermen. "You wouldn't be having us on, would you?" one of the policemen said.

"I swear it!" cried Willy. "It's the gospel truth! There's this little boy riding high up on the old turtle's back and his feet isn't even touching the water! He's dry as a bone and sitting there comfy and easy as could be! So we go after them. Of course we go after them. At first we try creeping up on them very quietly, like we always do when we're catching a turtle, but the boy sees us. We aren't very far away at this time, you understand. No more than from here to the edge of the water. And when the boy sees us, he sort of leans forward as if he's saying something to that old turtle, and the turtle's head comes up and he starts swimming like the clappers of hell! Man, could that turtle go! Tom and me can paddle pretty quick when we want to, but we've no chance against that monster! No chance at all! He's going at least twice as fast as we are! Easy twice as fast, what you say, Tom?"

"I'd say he's going *three times* as fast," Tom said. "And I'll

---

[1] energetically

tell you why. In about ten or fifteen minutes, they're a mile ahead of us."

"Why on earth didn't you call out to the boy?" the manager asked. "Why didn't you speak to him earlier on, when you were closer?"

"We never *stop* calling out, man!" Willy cried. "As soon as the boy sees us and we're not trying to creep up on them any longer, then we start yelling. We yell everything under the sun at that boy to try and get him aboard. 'Hey, boy!' I yell at him. 'You come on back with us! We'll give you a lift home! That ain't no good what you're doing there, boy! Jump off and swim while you got the chance and we'll pick you up! Go on boy, jump! Your mammy must be waiting for you at home, boy, so why don't you come on in with us?' And once I shouted at him. 'Listen, boy! We're gonna make you a promise! We promise not to catch that old turtle if you come with us!'"

"Did he answer you at all?" the manager asked.

"He never even looks round!" Willy said. "He sits high up on that shell and he's sort of rocking backwards and forwards with his body just like he's urging the old turtle to go faster and faster! You're gonna lose that little boy, Mr Edwards, unless someone gets out there real quick and grabs him away!"

The manager's normally pink face had turned white as paper. "Which way were they heading?" he asked sharply.

"North," Willy answered. "Almost due north."

"Right!" the manager said. "We'll take the speed-boat! I want you with us, Willy. And you, Tom."

The manager, the two policemen and the two fishermen ran down to where the boat that was used for water-skiing lay beached on the sand. They pushed the boat out, and even the manager lent a hand, wading up to his knees in his well-pressed white trousers. Then they all climbed in.

I watched them go zooming off.

Two hours later, I watched them coming back. They had seen nothing.

All through that day, speed-boats and yachts from other hotels along the coast searched the ocean. In the afternoon, the boy's father hired a helicopter. He rode in it himself and they were up there three hours. They found no trace of the turtle or the boy.

For a week, the search went on, but with no result.

And now, nearly a year has gone by since it happened. In that time, there has been only one significant[1] bit of news. A party of Americans, out from Nassau in the Bahamas, were deep-sea fishing off a large island called Eleuthera. There are literally thousands of coral reefs and small uninhabited islands in this area, and upon one of these tiny islands, the captain of the yacht saw through his binoculars the figure of a small person. There was a sandy beach on the island, and the small person was walking on the beach. The binoculars were passed around, and everyone who looked through them agreed that it was a child of some sort. There was, of course, a lot of excitement on board and the fishing lines were quickly reeled in. The captain steered the yacht straight for the island. When they were half a mile off, they were able, through the binoculars, to see clearly that the figure on the beach was a boy, and although sunburnt, he was almost certainly white-skinned, not a native. At that point, the watchers on the yacht also spotted what looked like a giant turtle on the sand near the boy. What happened next happened very quickly. The boy, who had probably caught sight of the approaching yacht, jumped on the turtle's back and the huge creature entered the water and swam at great speed around the island and out of sight. The yacht searched for two hours, but nothing more was seen either of the boy or the turtle.

There is no reason to disbelieve this report. There were five people on the yacht. Four of them were Americans and the captain was a Bahamian from Nassau. All of them in turn saw the boy and the turtle through the binoculars.

To reach Eleuthera Island from Jamaica by sea, one must first travel north-east for two hundred and fifty miles and pass through the Windward Passage between Cuba and Haiti. Then one must go north-north-west for a further three hundred miles at least. This is a total distance of five hundred and fifty miles, which is a very long journey for a small boy to make on the shell of a giant turtle.

Who knows what to think of all this?

One day, perhaps, he will come back, though I personally doubt it. I have a feeling he's quite happy where he is.

[1] meaningful

The Wish

The Wish

Under the palm of one hand the child became aware of the scab of an old cut on his kneecap. He bent forward to examine it closely. A scab was always a fascinating thing; it presented a special challenge he was never able to resist.

Yes, he thought, I will pick it off, even if it isn't ready, even if the middle of it sticks, even if it hurts like anything.

With a fingernail he began to explore cautiously around the edges of the scab. He got the nail underneath it, and when he raised it, but ever so slightly, it suddenly came off, the whole hard brown scab came off beautifully, leaving an interesting little circle of smooth red skin.

Nice. Very nice indeed. He rubbed the circle and it didn't hurt. He picked up the scab, put it on his thigh and flipped it with a finger so that it flew away and landed on the edge of the carpet, the enormous red and black and yellow carpet that stretched the whole length of the hall from the stairs on which he sat to the front door in the distance. A tremendous carpet. Bigger than the tennis lawn. Much bigger than that. He regarded it gravely, settling his eyes upon it with mild pleasure. He had never really noticed it before, but now, all of a sudden, the colours seemed to brighten mysteriously and spring out at him in a most dazzling way.

You see, he told himself, I know how it is. The red parts of the carpet are red-hot lumps of coal. What I must do is this: I must walk all the way along it to the front door without touching them. If I touch the red I will be burnt. As a matter of fact, I will be burnt up completely. And the black parts of the carpet . . . yes, the black parts are snakes, poisonous snakes, adders mostly, and cobras, thick like tree-trunks round the middle, and if I touch one of *them*, I'll be bitten and I'll die before tea time. And if I get across safely, without being burnt and without being bitten, I will be given a puppy for my birthday tomorrow.

He got to his feet and climbed higher up the stairs to obtain a better view of this vast tapestry of colour and death. Was it possible? Was there enough yellow? Yellow was the only colour he was allowed to walk on. Could it be done? This was not a journey to be undertaken lightly; the risks were too great for that. The child's face – a fringe of white-gold hair, two large blue eyes, a small pointed chin – peered down anxiously over the banisters. The yellow was a bit thin in places and there were one or two widish gaps, but it did seem to go all the way along to the other end. For someone who had only yesterday triumphantly travelled the whole length of the brick path from the stables to the summer-house without touching the cracks, this carpet thing should not be too difficult. Except for the snakes. The mere thought of snakes sent a fine electricity of fear running like pins down the backs of his legs and under the soles of his feet.

He came slowly down the stairs and advanced to the edge of the carpet. He extended one small sandalled foot and placed it cautiously upon a patch of yellow. Then he brought the other foot up, and there was just enough room for him to stand with the two feet together. There! He had started! His bright oval face was curiously intent, a shade whiter perhaps than before, and he was holding his arms out sideways to assist his balance. He took another step, lifting his foot high over a patch of black, aiming carefully with his toe for a narrow channel of yellow on the other side. When he had completed the second step he paused to rest, standing very stiff and still. The narrow channel of yellow ran forward unbroken for at least five yards and he advanced gingerly along it, bit by bit, as though walking a tightrope. Where it finally curled off sideways, he had to take another long stride, this time over a vicious-looking mixture of black and red. Half-way across he began to wobble. He waved his arms around wildly, windmill fashion, to keep his balance, and he got across safely and rested again on the other side. He was quite breathless now, and so tense he stood high on his toes all the time, arms out sideways, fists clenched. He was on a big safe island of yellow. There was lots of room on it, he couldn't possibly fall off, and he stood there resting, hesitating, waiting, wishing he could stay for ever on this big safe yellow island. But the fear of not getting the puppy compelled him to go on.

Step by step, he edged further ahead, and between each one he paused to decide exactly where next he should put his foot.

Once, he had a choice of ways, either to left or right, and he chose the left because although it seemed the more difficult, there was not so much black in that direction. The black was what made him nervous. He glanced quickly over his shoulder to see how far he had come. Nearly half-way. There could be no turning back now. He was in the middle and he couldn't turn back and he couldn't jump off sideways either because it was too far, and when he looked at all the red and all the black that lay ahead of him, he felt that old sudden sickening surge of panic in his chest – like last Easter time, that afternoon when he got lost all alone in the darkest part of Piper's Wood.

He took another step, placing his foot carefully upon the only little piece of yellow within reach, and this time the point of the foot came within a centimetre of some black. It wasn't touching the black, he could see it wasn't touching, he could see the small line of yellow separating the toe of his sandal from the black; but the snake stirred as though sensing the nearness, and raised its head and gazed at the foot with bright beady eyes, watching to see if it was going to touch.

"I'm not touching you! You mustn't bite me! You know I'm not touching you!"

Another snake slid up noiselessly beside the first, raised its head, two heads now, two pairs of eyes staring at the foot, gazing at a little naked place just below the sandal strap where the skin showed through. The child went high up on his toes and stayed there, frozen stiff with terror. It was minutes before he dared to move again.

The next step would have to be a really long one. There was this deep curling river of black that ran clear across the width of the carpet, and he was forced by this position to cross it at its widest part. He thought first of trying to jump it, but decided he couldn't be sure of landing accurately on the narrow band of yellow the other side. He took a deep breath, lifted one foot, and inch by inch he pushed it out in front of him, far far out, then down and down until at last the tip of his sandal was across and resting safely on the edge of the yellow. He leaned forward, transferring his weight to his front foot. Then he tried to bring the back foot up as well. He strained and pulled and jerked his body, but the legs were too wide apart and he couldn't make it. He tried to get back again. He couldn't do that either. He was doing the splits and he was properly stuck. He glanced down and saw this deep curling river of black underneath him. Parts of it were stirring now, and uncoiling and sliding and beginning to shine with a dreadfully oily glister. He wobbled, waved his arms frantically to keep his balance, but that seemed to make it worse. He was starting to go over. He was going over to the right, quite slowly he was going over, then faster and faster, and at the last moment, instinctively he put out a hand to break the fall and the next thing he saw was this bare hand of his going right into the middle of a great glistening mass of black and he gave one piercing cry of terror as it touched.

Outside in the sunshine, far away behind the house, the mother was looking for her son.

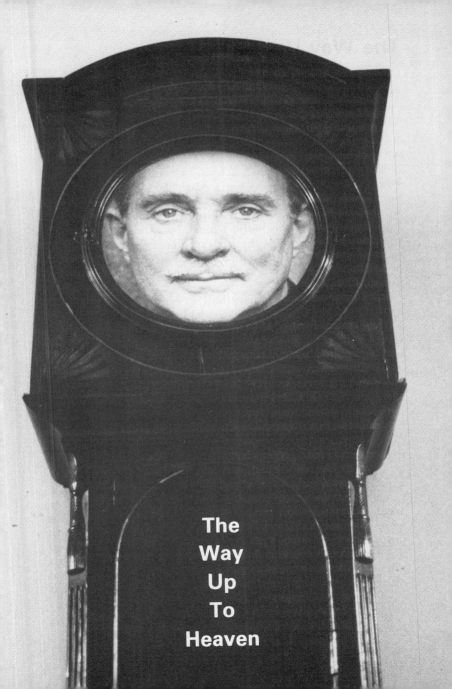

The
Way
Up
To
Heaven

The Way Up To Heaven

All her life, Mrs Foster had had an almost pathological[1] fear of missing a train, a plane, a boat, or even a theatre curtain. In other respects, she was not a particularly nervous woman, but the mere thought of being late on occasions like these would throw her into such a state of nerves that she would begin to twitch. It was nothing much – just a tiny vellicating[2] muscle in the corner of the left eye, like a secret wink – but the annoying thing was that it refused to disappear until an hour or so after the train or plane or whatever it was had been safely caught.

It was really extraordinary how in certain people a simple apprehension about a thing like catching a train can grow into a serious obsession. At least half an hour before it was time to leave the house for the station, Mrs Foster would step out of the elevator all ready to go, with hat and coat and gloves, and then, being quite unable to sit down, she would flutter and fidget about from room to room until her husband, who must have been well aware of her state, finally emerged from his privacy and suggested in a cool dry voice that perhaps they had better get going now, had they not?

Mr Foster may possibly have had a right to be irritated by this foolishness of his wife's, but he could have had no excuse for increasing her misery by keeping her waiting unnecessarily. Mind you, it is by no means certain that this is what he did, yet whenever they were to go somewhere, his timing was so accurate – just a minute or two late, you understand – and his manner so bland that it was hard to believe he wasn't purposely inflicting a nasty private little torture of his own on the unhappy lady. And one thing he must have known – that she would never dare to call out and tell him to hurry. He had disciplined her too well for that. He must also have known that

---

[1] unhealthy
[2] twitching

if he was prepared to wait even beyond the last moment of safety, he could drive her nearly into hysterics. On one or two special occasions in the later years of their married life, it seemed almost as though he had *wanted* to miss the train simply in order to intensify the poor woman's suffering.

Assuming (though one cannot be sure) that the husband was guilty, what made his attitude doubly unreasonable was the fact that, with the exception of this one small irrepressible[1] foible,[2] Mrs Foster was and always had been a good and loving wife. For over thirty years, she had served him loyally and well. There was no doubt about this. Even she, a very modest woman, was aware of it, and although she had for years refused to let herself believe that Mr Foster would ever consciously torment her, there had been times recently when she had caught herself beginning to wonder.

Mr Eugene Foster, who was nearly seventy years old, lived with his wife in a large six-storey house in New York City, on East Sixty-second Street, and they had four servants. It was a gloomy place, and few people came to visit them. But on this particular morning in January, the house had come alive and there was a great deal of bustling about. One maid was distributing bundles of dust sheets to every room, while another was draping them over the furniture. The butler was bringing down suitcases and putting them in the hall. The cook kept popping up from the kitchen to have a word with the butler, and Mrs Foster herself, in an old-fashioned fur coat and with a black hat on the top of her head, was flying from room to room and pretending to supervise these operations. Actually, she was thinking of nothing at all except that she was going to miss her plane if her husband didn't come out of his study soon and get ready.

"What time is it, Walker?" she said to the butler as she passed him.

"It's ten minutes past nine, Madam."

"And has the car come?"

"Yes, Madam, it's waiting, I'm just going to put the luggage in now."

"It takes an hour to get to Idlewild," she said. "My plane leaves at eleven. I have to be there half an hour beforehand

[1]   not to be put down
[2]   weakness

for the formalities. I shall be late. I just *know* I'm going to be late."

"I think you have plenty of time, Madam," the butler said kindly. "I warned Mr Foster that you must leave at nine-fifteen. There's still another five minutes."

"Yes, Walker, I know, I know. But get the luggage in quickly, will you please?"

She began walking up and down the hall, and whenever the butler came by, she asked him the time. This, she kept telling herself, was the *one* plane she must not miss. It had taken months to persuade her husband to allow her to go. If she missed it, he might easily decide that she should cancel the whole thing. And the trouble was that he insisted on coming to the airport to see her off.

"Dear God," she said aloud, "I'm going to miss it. I know, I know, I *know* I'm going to miss it." The little muscle beside the left eye was twitching madly now. The eyes themselves were very close to tears.

"What time is it, Walker?"

"It's eighteen minutes past, Madam."

"Now I really *will* miss it!" she cried. "Oh, I wish he would come!"

This was an important journey for Mrs Foster. She was going all alone to Paris to visit her daughter, her only child, who was married to a Frenchman. Mrs Foster didn't care much for the Frenchman, but she was fond of her daughter, and, more than that, she had developed a great yearning to set eyes on her three grandchildren. She knew them only from the many photographs that she had received and that she kept putting up all over the house. They were beautiful, these children. She doted on them, and each time a new picture arrived she would carry it away and sit with it for a long time, staring at it lovingly and searching the small faces for signs of that old satisfying blood likeness that meant so much. And now, lately, she had come more and more to feel that she did not really wish to live out her days in a place where she could not be near these children, and have them visit her, and take them for walks, and buy them presents, and watch them grow. She knew, of course, that it was wrong and in a way disloyal to have thoughts like these while her husband was still alive. She knew also that although he was no longer active in his many enterprises, he would never consent to leave New York and live

in Paris. It was a miracle that he had ever agreed to let her
fly over there alone for six weeks to visit them. But, oh, how
she wished she could live there always, and be close to them!

"Walker, what time is it?"

"Twenty-two minutes past, Madam."

As he spoke, a door opened and Mr Foster came into the
hall. He stood for a moment, looking intently at his wife, and
she looked back at him – at this diminutive[1] but still quite
dapper old man with the huge bearded face that bore such an
astonishing resemblance to those old photographs of Andrew
Carnegie.

"Well," he said, "I suppose perhaps we'd better get going
fairly soon if you want to catch that plane."

"*Yes*, dear – *yes!* Everything's ready. The car's waiting."

"That's good," he said. With his head over to one side, he
was watching her closely. He had a peculiar way of cocking
the head and then moving it in a series of small, rapid jerks.
Because of this and because he was clasping his hands up high
in front of him, near the chest, he was somehow like a squirrel
standing there – a quick clever old squirrel from the Park.

"Here's Walker with your coat, dear. Put it on."

"I'll be with you in a moment," he said. "I'm just going to
wash my hands."

She waited for him, and the tall butler stood beside her,
holding the coat and the hat.

"Walker, will I miss it?"

"No, Madam," the butler said. "I think you'll make it all
right."

Then Mr Foster appeared again, and the butler helped him
on with his coat. Mrs Foster hurried outside and got into the
hired Cadillac. Her husband came after her, but he walked
down the steps of the house slowly, pausing halfway to observe
the sky and to sniff the cold morning air.

"It looks a bit foggy," he said as he sat down beside her in
the car. "And it's always worse out there at the airport. I
shouldn't be surprised if the flight's cancelled already."

"Don't say that, dear – *please*."

They didn't speak again until the car had crossed over the
river to Long Island.

"I arranged everything with the servants," Mr Foster said.

[1] small

"They're all going off today. I gave them half-pay for six weeks and told Walker I'd send him a telegram when we wanted them back."

"Yes," she said. "He told me."

"I'll move into the club tonight. It'll be a nice change staying at the club."

"Yes, dear. I'll write to you."

"I'll call in at the house occasionally to see that everything's all right and to pick up the mail.

"But don't you really think Walker should stay there all the time to look after things?" she asked meekly.

"Nonsense. It's quite unnecessary. And anyway, I'd have to pay him full wages."

"Oh yes," she said. "Of course."

"What's more, you never know what people get up to when they're left alone in a house," Mr Foster announced, and with that he took out a cigar and, after snipping off the end with a silver cutter, lit it with a gold lighter.

She sat still in the car with her hands clasped together tight under the rug.

"Will you write to me?" she asked.

"I'll see," he said. "But I doubt it. You know I don't hold with letter-writing unless there's something specific to say."

"Yes, dear, I know. So don't you bother."

They drove on, along Queen's Boulevard, and as they approached the flat marshland on which Idlewild is built, the fog began to thicken and the car had to slow down.

"Oh dear!" cried Mrs Foster. "I'm *sure* I'm going to miss it now! What time is it?"

"Stop fussing," the old man said. "It doesn't matter anyway. It's bound to be cancelled now. They never fly in this sort of weather. I don't know why you bothered to come out."

She couldn't be sure, but it seemed to her that there was suddenly a new note in his voice, and she turned to look at him. It was difficult to observe any change in his expression under all that hair. The mouth was what counted. She wished, as she had so often before, that she could see the mouth clearly. The eyes never showed anything except when he was in a rage.

"Of course," he went on, "if by any chance it *does* go, then I agree with you – you'll be certain to miss it now. Why don't you resign yourself to that?"

She turned away and peered through the window at the fog. It seemed to be getting thicker as they went along, and now she could only just make out the edge of the road and the margin of grassland beyond it. She knew that her husband was still looking at her. She glanced at him again, and this time she noticed with a kind of horror that he was staring intently at the little place in the corner of her left eye where she could feel the muscle twitching.

"Won't you?" he said.

"Won't I what?"

"Be sure to miss it now if it goes. We can't drive fast in this muck."

He didn't speak to her any more after that. The car crawled on and on. The driver had a yellow lamp directed on to the edge of the road, and this helped him to keep going. Other lights, some white and some yellow, kept coming out of the fog towards them, and there was an especially bright one that followed close behind them all the time.

Suddenly, the driver stopped the car.

"There!" Mr Foster cried. "We're stuck. I knew it."

"No, sir," the driver said, turning round. "We made it. This is the airport."

Without a word, Mrs Foster jumped out and hurried through the main entrance into the building. There was a mass of people inside, mostly disconsolate passengers standing around the ticket counters. She pushed her way through and spoke to the clerk.

"Yes," he said. "Your flight is temporarily postponed. But please don't go away. We're expecting this weather to clear any moment."

She went back to her husband who was still sitting in the car and told him the news. "But don't you wait, dear," she said. "There's no sense in that."

"I won't," he answered. "So long as the driver can get me back. Can you get me back, driver?"

"I think so," the man said.

"Is the luggage out?"

"Yes, sir."

"Good-bye, dear," Mrs Foster said, leaning into the car and giving her husband a small kiss on the coarse grey fur of his cheek.

"Good-bye," he answered. "Have a good trip."

The car drove off, and Mrs Foster was left alone.

The rest of the day was a sort of nightmare for her. She sat for hour after hour on a bench, as close to the airline counter as possible, and every thirty minutes or so she would get up and ask the clerk if the situation had changed. She always received the same reply – that she must continue to wait, because the fog might blow away at any moment. It wasn't until after six in the evening that the loudspeakers finally announced that the flight had been postponed until eleven o'clock the next morning.

Mrs Foster didn't quite know what to do when she heard this news. She stayed sitting on her bench for at least another half-hour, wondering, in a tired, hazy sort of way, where she might go to spend the night. She hated to leave the airport. She didn't wish to see her husband. She was terrified that in one way or another he would eventually manage to prevent her from getting to France. She would have liked to remain just where she was, sitting on the bench the whole night through. That would be the safest. But she was already exhausted, and it didn't take her long to realize that this was a ridiculous thing for an elderly lady to do. So in the end she went to a phone and called the house.

Her husband, who was on the point of leaving for the club, answered it himself. She told him the news, and asked whether the servants were still there.

"They've all gone," he said.

"In that case, dear, I'll just get myself a room somewhere for the night. And don't you bother yourself about it at all."

"That would be foolish," he said. "You've got a large house here at your disposal. Use it."

"But, dear, it's *empty*."

"Then I'll stay with you myself."

"There's no food in the house. There's nothing."

"Then eat before you come in. Don't be so stupid, woman. Everything you do, you seem to want to make a fuss about it."

"Yes," she said. "I'm sorry. I'll get myself a sandwich here, and then I'll come on in."

Outside, the fog had cleared a little, but it was still a long, slow drive in the taxi, and she didn't arrive back at the house on Sixty-second Street until fairly late.

Her husband emerged from his study when he heard her

coming in. "Well," he said, standing by the study door, "how was Paris?"

"We leave at eleven in the morning," she answered. "It's definite."

"You mean if the fog clears."

"It's clearing now. There's a wind coming up."

"You look tired," he said. "You must have had an anxious day."

"It wasn't very comfortable. I think I'll go straight to bed."

"I've ordered a car for the morning," he said. "Nine o'clock."

"Oh, thank you, dear. And I certainly hope you're not going to bother to come all the way out again to see me off."

"No," he said slowly. "I don't think I will. But there's no reason why you shouldn't drop me at the club on your way."

She looked at him, and at that moment he seemed to be standing a long way off from her, beyond some borderline. He was suddenly so small and far away that she couldn't be sure what he was doing, or what he was thinking, or even what he was.

"The club is downtown," she said. "It isn't on the way to the airport."

"But you'll have plenty of time, my dear. Don't you want to drop me at the club?"

"Oh, yes – of course."

"That's good. Then I'll see you in the morning at nine."

She went up to her bedroom on the second floor, and she was so exhausted from her day that she fell asleep soon after she lay down.

Next morning, Mrs Foster was up early, and by eight-thirty she was downstairs and ready to leave.

Shortly after nine, her husband appeared. "Did you make any coffee?" he asked.

"No, dear. I though you'd get a nice breakfast at the club. The car is here. It's been waiting. I'm all ready to go."

They were standing in the hall – they always seemed to be meeting in the hall nowadays – she with her hat and coat and purse, he in a curiously cut Edwardian jacket with high lapels.

"Your luggage?"

"It's at the airport."

"Ah yes," he said. "Of course. And if you're going to take

me to the club first, I suppose we'd better get going fairly soon, hadn't we?"

"Yes!" she cried. "Oh, yes – *please!*"

"I'm just going to get a few cigars. I'll be right with you. You get in the car."

She turned and went out to where the chauffeur was standing, and he opened the car door for her as she approached.

"What time is it?" she asked him.

"About nine-fifteen."

Mr Foster came out five minutes later, and watching him as he walked slowly down the steps, she noticed that his legs were like goat's legs in those narrow stovepipe trousers that he wore. As on the day before, he paused half-way down to sniff the air and to examine the sky. The weather was still not quite clear, but there was a wisp of sun coming through the mist.

"Perhaps you'll be lucky this time," he said as he settled himself beside her in the car.

"Hurry, please," she said to the chauffeur. "Don't bother about the rug. I'll arrange the rug. Please get going. I'm late."

The man went back to his seat behind the wheel and started the engine.

"*Just* a moment!" Mr Foster said suddenly. "Hold it a moment, chauffeur, will you?"

"What is it, dear?" She saw him searching the pockets of his overcoat.

"I had a little present I wanted you to take to Ellen," he said. "Now, where on earth is it? I'm sure I had it in my hand as I came down."

"I never saw you carrying anything. What sort of present?"

"A little box wrapped up in white paper. I forgot to give it to you yesterday. I don't want to forget it today."

"A little box!" Mrs Foster cried. "I never saw any little box!" She began hunting frantically in the back of the car.

Her husband continued searching through the pockets of his coat. Then he unbuttoned the coat and felt around in his jacket. "Confound it," he said, "I must've left it in my bedroom. I won't be a moment."

"Oh, *please!*" she cried. "We haven't got time! *Please* leave it! You can mail it. It's only one of those silly combs anyway. You're always giving her combs."

"And what's wrong with combs, may I ask?" he said, furious that she should have forgotten herself for once.

"Nothing, dear, I'm sure. But . . ."

"Stay here!" he commanded. "I'm going to get it."

"Be quick, dear! Oh, *please* be quick!"

She sat still, waiting and waiting.

"Chauffeur, what time is it?"

The man had a wristwatch, which he consulted. "I make it nearly nine-thirty."

"Can we get to the airport in an hour?"

"Just about."

At this point, Mrs Foster suddenly spotted a corner of something white wedged down in the crack of the seat on the side where her husband had been sitting. She reached over and pulled out a small paper-wrapped box, and at the same time she couldn't help noticing that it was wedged down firm and deep, as though with the help of a pushing hand.

"Here it is!" she cried. "I've found it! Oh dear, and now he'll be up there for ever searching for it! Chauffeur, quickly – run in and call him down, will you please?"

The chauffeur, a man with a small rebellious Irish mouth, didn't care very much for any of this, but he climbed out of the car and went up the steps to the front door of the house. Then he turned and came back. "Door's locked," he announced. "You got a key?"

"Yes – wait a minute." She began hunting madly in her purse. The little face was screwed up tight with anxiety, the lips pushed outward like a spout.

"Here it is! No – I'll go myself. It'll be quicker. I know where he'll be."

She hurried out of the car and up the steps to the front door, holding the key in one hand. She slid the key into the keyhole and was about to turn it – and then she stopped. Her head came up, and she stood there absolutely motionless, her whole body arrested right in the middle of all this hurry to turn the key and get into the house, and she waited – five, six, seven, eight, nine, ten seconds, she waited. The way she was standing there, with her head in the air and the body so tense, it seemed as though she were listening for the repetition of some sound that she had heard a moment before from a place far away inside the house.

Yes – quite obviously she was listening. Her whole attitude

was a *listening* one. She appeared actually to be moving one of her ears closer and closer to the door. Now it was right up against the door, and for still another few seconds she remained in that position, head up, ear to door, hand on key, about to enter but not entering, trying instead, or so it seemed, to hear and to analyse these sounds that were coming faintly from this place deep within the house.

Then, all at once, she sprang to life again. She withdrew the key from the door and came running back down the steps.

"It's too late!" she cried to the chauffeur. "I can't wait for him, I simply can't. I'll miss the plane. Hurry now, driver, hurry! To the airport!"

The chauffeur, had he been watching her closely, might have noticed that her face had turned absolutely white and that the whole expression had suddenly altered. There was no longer that rather soft and silly look. A peculiar hardness had settled itself upon the features. The little mouth, usually so flabby, was now tight and thin, the eyes were bright, and the voice, when she spoke, carried a new note of authority.

"Hurry, driver, hurry!"

"Isn't your husband travelling with you?" the man asked, astonished.

"Certainly not! I was only going to drop him at the club. It won't matter. He'll understand. He'll get a cab. Don't sit there talking, man. *Get going!* I've got a plane to catch for Paris!"

With Mrs Foster urging him from the back seat, the man drove fast all the way, and she caught her plane with a few minutes to spare. Soon she was high up over the Atlantic, reclining comfortably in her aeroplane chair, listening to the hum of the motors, heading for Paris at last. The new mood was still with her. She felt remarkably strong and, in a queer sort of way, wonderful. She was a trifle breathless with it all, but this was more from pure astonishment at what she had done than anything else, and as the plane flew farther and farther away from New York and East Sixty-second Street, a great sense of calmness began to settle upon her. By the time she reached Paris, she was just as strong and cool and calm as she could wish.

She met her grandchildren, and they were even more beautiful in the flesh than in their photographs. They were like angels, she told herself, so beautiful they were. And every day she took them for walks, and fed them cakes, and bought them presents, and told them charming stories.

Once a week, on Tuesdays, she wrote a letter to her husband – a nice, chatty letter – full of news and gossip, which always ended with the words "Now be sure to take your meals regularly, dear, although this is something I'm afraid you may not be doing when I'm not with you."

When the six weeks were up, everybody was sad that she had to return to America, to her husband. Everybody, that is, except her. Surprisingly, she didn't seem to mind as much as one might have expected, and when she kissed them all good-bye, there was something in her manner and in the things she said that appeared to hint at the possibility of a return in the not too distant future.

However, like the faithful wife she was, she did not overstay her time. Exactly six weeks after she had arrived, she sent a cable to her husband and caught the plane back to New York.

Arriving at Idlewild, Mrs Foster was interested to observe that there was no car to meet her. It is possible that she might even have been a little amused. But she was extremely calm and did not overtip the porter who helped her into a taxi with her baggage.

New York was colder than Paris, and there were lumps of dirty snow lying in the gutters of the streets. The taxi drew up before the house on Sixty-second Street, and Mrs Foster persuaded the driver to carry her two large cases to the top of the steps. Then she paid him off and rang the bell. She waited, but there was no answer. Just to make sure, she rang again, and she could hear it tinkling shrilly far away in the pantry, at the back of the house. But still no one came.

So she took out her own key and opened the door herself.

The first thing she saw as she entered was a great pile of mail lying on the floor where it had fallen after being slipped through the letter box. The place was dark and cold. A dust sheet was still draped over the grandfather clock. In spite of the cold, the atmosphere was peculiarly oppressive, and there was a faint and curious odour in the air that she had never smelled before.

She walked quickly across the hall and disappeared for a moment around the corner to the left, at the back. There was something deliberate and purposeful about this action; she had the air of a woman who is off to investigate a rumour or to confirm a suspicion. And when she returned a few seconds later, there was a little glimmer of satisfaction on her face.

She paused in the centre of the hall, as though wondering what to do next. Then, suddenly, she turned and went across into her husband's study. On the desk she found his address book, and after hunting through it for a while she picked up the phone and dialled a number.

"Hello," she said. "Listen – this is Nine East Sixty-second Street. . . Yes, that's right. Could you send someone round as soon as possible, do you think? Yes, it seems to be stuck between the second and third floors. At least, that's where the indicator's pointing. . . Right away? Oh, that's very kind of you. You see, my legs aren't any too good for walking up a lot of stairs. Thank you so much. Good-bye."

She replaced the receiver and sat there at her husband's desk, patiently waiting for the man who would be coming soon to repair the lift.

Royal Jelly

Royal Jelly

"It worries me to death, Albert, it really does," Mrs Taylor said.

She kept her eyes fixed on the baby who was now lying absolutely motionless in the crook of her left arm.

"I just know there's something wrong."

The skin on the baby's face had a pearly translucent quality and was stretched very tightly over the bones.

"Try again," Albert Taylor said.

"It won't do any good."

"You have to keep trying, Mabel," he said.

She lifted the bottle out of the saucepan of hot water and shook a few drops of milk on to the inside of her wrist, testing for temperature.

"Come on," she whispered. "Come on, my baby. Wake up and take a bit more of this."

There was a small lamp on the table close by that made a soft yellow glow all around her.

"Please," she said. "Take just a weeny bit more."

The husband watched her over the top of his magazine. She was half dead with exhaustion, he could see that, and the pale oval face, usually so grave and serene, had taken on a kind of pinched and desperate look. But even so, the drop of her head as she gazed down at the child was curiously beautiful.

"You see," she murmured. "It's no good. She won't have it."

She held the bottle up to the light, squinting at the calibrations.[1]

"One ounce again. That's all she's taken. No – it isn't even that. It's only three-quarters. It's not enough to keep body and soul together, Albert, it really isn't. It worries me to death."

"I know," he said.

"If only they could *find out* what was wrong."

[1] Scale of readings

"There's nothing wrong, Mabel. It's just a matter of time."

"Of course there's something wrong."

"Dr Robinson says no."

"Look," she said, standing up. "You can't tell me it's natural for a six-week-old child to weigh less, less by more than *two whole pounds* than she did when she was born! Just look at those legs! They're nothing but skin and bone!"

The tiny baby lay limply on her arm, not moving.

"Dr Robinson said you was to stop worrying, Mabel. So did that other one."

"Ha!" she said. "Isn't that wonderful! I'm to stop worrying!"

"Now, Mabel."

"What does he want me to do? Treat it as some sort of a joke?"

"He didn't say that."

"I hate doctors! I hate them all!" she cried, and she swung away from him and walked quickly out of the room towards the stairs, carrying the baby with her.

Albert Taylor stayed where he was and let her go.

In a little while he heard her moving about in the bedroom directly over his head, quick nervous footsteps going tap tap tap on the linoleum above. Soon the footsteps would stop, and then he would have to get up and follow her, and when he went into the bedroom he would find her sitting beside the cot as usual, staring at the child and crying softly to herself and refusing to move.

"She's starving, Albert," she would say.

"Of course she's not starving."

"She *is* starving. I know she is. And Albert?"

"Yes?"

"I believe you know it too, but you won't admit it. Isn't that right?"

Every night now it was like this.

Last week they had taken the child back to the hospital, and the doctor had examined it carefully and told them that there was nothing the matter.

"It took us nine years to get this baby, Doctor," Mabel had said. "I think it would kill me if anything should happen to her."

That was six days ago and since then it had lost another five ounces.

But worrying about it wasn't going to help anybody, Albert Taylor told himself. One simply had to trust the doctor on a thing like this. He picked up the magazine that was still lying on his lap and glanced idly down the list of contents to see what it had to offer this week:

Among the Bees in May
Honey Cookery
The Bee Farmer and the B. Pharm.
Experiences in the Control of Nosema
The Latest on Royal Jelly
This Week in the Apiary
The Healing Power of Propolis
Regurgitations
British Beekeepers Annual Dinner
Association News

All his life Albert Taylor had been fascinated by anything that had to do with bees. As a small boy he used often to catch them in his bare hands and go running with them into the house to show to his mother, and sometimes he would put them on his face and let them crawl about over his cheeks and neck, and the astonishing thing about it all was that he never got stung. On the contrary, the bees seemed to enjoy being with him. They never tried to fly away, and to get rid of them he would have to brush them off gently with his fingers. Even then they would frequently return and settle again on his arm or hand or knee, any place where the skin was bare.

His father, who was a bricklayer, said there must be some witch's stench about the boy, something noxious that came oozing out through the pores of the skin, and that no good would ever come of it, hypnotizing insects like that. But the mother said it was a gift given him by God, and even went so far as to compare him with St Francis and the birds.

As he grew older, Albert Taylor's fascination with bees developed into an obsession, and by the time he was twelve he had built his first hive. The following summer he had captured his first swarm. Two years later, at the age of fourteen, he had no less than five hives standing neatly in a row against the fence in his father's small back yard, and already – apart from the normal task of producing honey – he was practising the delicate and complicated business of rearing his own queens, grafting larvae[1] into artificial cell cups, and all the rest of it.

He never had to use smoke when there was work to do inside a hive, and he never wore gloves on his hands or a net over his head. Clearly there was some strange sympathy between this boy and the bees, and down in the village, in the shops and pubs, they began to speak about him with a certain kind of respect, and people started coming up to the house to buy his honey.

When he was eighteen, he had rented one acre of rough pasture alongside a cherry orchard down the valley about a mile from the village, and there he had set out to establish his own business. Now, eleven years later, he was still in the same spot, but he had six acres of ground instead of one, two hundred and forty well-stocked hives, and a small house that he'd built mainly with his own hands. He had married at the age of twenty and that, apart from the fact that it had taken them over nine years to get a child, had also been a success. In fact, everything had gone pretty well for Albert until this strange little baby girl came along and started frightening them out of their wits by refusing to eat properly and losing weight every day.

He looked up from the magazine and began thinking about his daughter.

That evening, for instance, when she had opened her eyes at the beginning of the feed, he had gazed into them and seen something that frightened him to death – a kind of misty vacant stare, as though the eyes themselves were not connected to the brain at all but were just lying loose in their sockets like a couple of small grey marbles.

Did those doctors really know what they were talking about?

He reached for an ash-tray and started slowly picking the ashes out from the bowl of his pipe with a matchstick.

One could always take her along to another hospital, somewhere in Oxford perhaps. He might suggest that to Mabel when he went upstairs.

He could still hear her moving around in the bedroom, but she must have taken off her shoes now and put on slippers because the noise was very faint.

He switched his attention back to the magazine and went

---

[1] bees in the stage between egg and pupa

on with his reading. He finished the article called "Experiences in the Control of Nosema", then turned over the page and began reading the next one, "The Latest on Royal Jelly". He doubted very much whether there would be anything in this that he didn't know already:

What is the wonderful substance called royal jelly?

He reached for the tin of tobacco on the table beside him and began filling his pipe, still reading.

Royal jelly is a glandular secretion produced by the nurse bees to feed the larvae immediately they have hatched from the egg. The pharyngeal glands of bees produce this substance in much the same way as the mammary glands of vertebrates produce milk. The fact is of great biological interest because no other insects in the world are known to have evolved such a process.

All old stuff, he told himself, but for want of anything better to do, he continued to read.

Royal jelly is fed in concentrated form to all bee larvae for the first three days after hatching from the egg; but beyond that point, for all those who are destined to become drones or workers, this precious food is greatly diluted with honey and pollen. On the other hand, the larvae which are destined to become queens are fed throughout the whole of their larval period on a concentrated diet of pure royal jelly. Hence the name.

Above him, up in the bedroom, the noise of the footsteps had stopped altogether. The house was quiet. He struck a match and put it to his pipe.

Royal jelly must be a substance of tremendous nourishing power, for on this diet alone, the honey-bee larva increases in weight fifteen hundred times in five days.

That was probably about right, he thought, although for some reason it had never occurred to him to consider larval growth in terms of weight before.

This is as if a seven-and-a-half-pound baby should increase in that time to five tons.

Albert Taylor stopped and read that sentence again.
He read it a third time.

This is as if a seven-and-a-half-pound baby . . .

"Mabel!" he cried, jumping up from his chair. "Mabel! come here!"

He went out into the hall and stood at the foot of the stairs calling for her to come down.
There was no answer.
He ran up the stairs and switched on the light on the landing. The bedroom door was closed. He crossed the landing and opened it and stood in the doorway looking into the dark room. "Mabel," he said. "Come downstairs a moment, will you please? I've just had a bit of an idea. It's about the baby."
The light from the landing behind him cast a faint glow over the bed and he could see her dimly now, lying on her stomach with her face buried in the pillow and her arms up over her head. She was crying again.
"Mabel," he said, going over to her, touching her shoulder. "Please come down a moment. This may be important."
"Go away," she said. "Leave me alone."
"Don't you want to hear about my idea?"
"Oh, Albert, I'm *tired*," she sobbed. "I'm so tired I don't know what I'm doing any more. I don't think I can go on. I don't think I can stand it."
There was a pause. Albert Taylor turned away from her and walked slowly over to the cradle where the baby was lying, and peered in. It was too dark for him to see the child's face, but when he bent down close he could hear the sound of breathing, very faint and quick. "What time is the next feed?" he asked.
"Two o'clock, I suppose."
"And the one after that?"
"Six in the morning."
"I'll do them both," he said. "You go to sleep."
She didn't answer.
"You get properly into bed, Mabel, and go straight to sleep, you understand? And stop worrying. I'm taking over

completely for the next twelve hours. You'll give yourself a nervous breakdown going on like this."

"Yes," she said. "I know."

"I'm taking the nipper and myself *and* the alarm clock into the spare room this very moment, so you just lie down and relax and forget all about us. Right?" Already he was pushing the cradle out through the door.

"Oh, Albert," she sobbed.

"Don't you worry about a thing. Leave it to me."

"Albert . . ."

"Yes?"

"I love you, Albert."

"I love you too, Mabel. Now go to sleep."

Albert Taylor didn't see his wife again until nearly eleven o'clock the next morning.

"Good *gracious* me!" she cried, rushing down the stairs in dressing-gown and slippers. "Albert! Just look at the time! I must have slept twelve hours at least! Is everything all right? What happened?"

He was sitting quietly in his armchair, smoking a pipe and reading the morning paper. The baby was in a sort of carry-cot on the floor at his feet, sleeping.

"Hullo, dear," he said, smiling.

She ran over to the cot and looked in. "Did she take anything, Albert? How many times have you fed her? She was due for another one at ten o'clock, did you know that?"

Albert Taylor folded the newspaper neatly into a square and put it away on the side table. "I fed her at two in the morning," he said, "and she took about half an ounce, no more. I fed her again at six and she did a bit better that time, two ounces . . ."

"*Two ounces!* Oh, Albert, that's marvellous!"

"And we just finished the last feed ten minutes ago. There's the bottle on the mantelpiece. Only one ounce left. She drank three. How's that?" He was grinning proudly, delighted with his achievement.

The woman quickly got down on her knees and peered at the baby.

"Don't she look better?" he asked eagerly. "Don't she look fatter in the face?"

"It may sound silly," the wife said, "but I actually think

she does. Oh, Albert, you're a marvel! How did you do it?"

"She's turning the corner," he said. "That's all it is. Just like the doctor prophesied, she's turning the corner."

"I pray to God you're right, Albert."

"Of course I'm right. From now on, you watch her go."

The woman was gazing lovingly at the baby.

"You look a lot better yourself too, Mabel."

"I feel wonderful. I'm sorry about last night."

"Let's keep it this way," he said. "I'll do all the night feeds in future. You do the day ones."

She looked up at him across the cot, frowning. "No," she said. "Oh no, I wouldn't allow you to do that."

"I don't want you to have a breakdown, Mabel."

"I won't, not now I've had some sleep."

"Much better we share it."

"No, Albert. This is my job and I intend to do it. Last night won't happen again."

There was a pause. Albert Taylor took the pipe out of his mouth and examined the grain on the bowl. "All right," he said. "In that case I'll just relieve you of the donkey work, I'll do all the sterilizing and the mixing of the food and getting everything ready. That'll help you a bit, anyway."

She looked at him carefully, wondering what could have come over him all of a sudden.

"You see, Mabel, I've never even raised a finger to help you with this baby."

"That isn't true."

"Oh yes it is. So I've decided that from now on I'm going to do *my* share of the work. I'm going to be the feed-mixer and the bottle-sterilizer. Right?"

"It's very sweet of you, dear, but I really don't think it's necessary. . ."

"Come on!" he cried. "Don't change the luck! I done it the last three times and just *look* what happened! When's the next one? Two o'clock, isn't it?"

"Yes."

"It's all mixed," he said. "Everything's all mixed and ready and all you've got to do when the time comes is to go out there to the larder and take it off the shelf and warm it up. That's *some* help, isn't it?"

The woman got up off her knees and went over to him and kissed him on the cheek. "You're such a nice man," she said. "I love you more and more every day I know you."

Later, in the middle of the afternoon, when Albert was outside in the sunshine working among the hives, he heard her calling to him from the house.

"Albert!" she shouted. "Albert, come here!" She was running through the buttercups towards him.

He started forward to meet her, wondering what was wrong.

"Oh, Albert! Guess what!"

"What?"

"I've just finished giving her the two-o'clock feed and she's taken the whole lot!"

"No!"

"Every drop of it! Oh, Albert, I'm so happy! She's going to be all right! She's turned the corner just like you said!" She came up to him and threw her arms around his neck and hugged him, and he clapped her on the back and laughed and said what a marvellous little mother she was.

"Will you come in and watch the next one and see if she does it again, Albert?"

He told her he wouldn't miss it for anything, and she hugged him again, then turned and ran back to the house, skipping over the grass and singing all the way.

Naturally, there was a certain amount of suspense in the air as the time approached for the six-o'clock feed. By five thirty both parents were already seated in the living-room waiting for the moment to arrive. The bottle with the milk formula in it was standing in a saucepan of warm water on the mantelpiece. The baby was asleep in its carry-cot on the sofa.

At twenty minutes to six it woke up and started screaming its head off.

"There you are!" Mrs Taylor cried. "She's asking for the bottle. Pick her up quick, Albert, and hand her to me here. Give me the bottle first."

He gave her the bottle, then placed the baby on the woman's lap. Cautiously, she touched the baby's lips with the end of the nipple. The baby seized the nipple between its gums and began to suck ravenously with a rapid powerful action.

"Oh, Albert, isn't it wonderful?" she said, laughing.

"It's terrific, Mabel."

In seven or eight minutes, the entire contents of the bottle had disappeared down the baby's throat.

"You clever girl," Mrs Taylor said. "Four ounces again."

Albert Taylor was leaning forward in his chair, peering intently into the baby's face. "You know what?" he said. "She even seems as though she's put on a touch of weight already. What do you think?"

The mother looked down at the child.

"Don't she seem bigger and fatter to you, Mabel, than she was yesterday?"

"Maybe she does, Albert. I'm not sure. Although actually there couldn't be any *real* gain in such a short time as this. The important thing is that she's eating normally."

"She's turned the corner," Albert said. "I don't think you need worry about her any more."

"I certainly won't."

"You want me to go up and fetch the cradle back into our own bedroom, Mabel?"

"Yes, please," she said.

Albert went upstairs and moved the cradle. The woman followed with the baby, and after changing its nappy, she laid it gently down on its bed. Then she covered it with sheet and blanket.

"Doesn't she look lovely, Albert?" she whispered. "Isn't that the most beautiful baby you've ever seen in your *entire* life?"

"Leave her be now, Mabel," he said. "Come on downstairs and cook us a bit of supper. We both deserve it."

After they had finished eating, the parents settled themselves in armchairs in the living-room, Albert with his magazine and his pipe, Mrs Taylor with her knitting. But this was a very different scene from the one of the night before. Suddenly, all tensions had vanished. Mrs Taylor's handsome oval face was glowing with pleasure, her cheeks were pink, her eyes were sparkling bright, and her mouth was fixed in a little dreamy smile of pure content. Every now and again she would glance up from her knitting and gaze affectionately at ther husband. Occasionally, she would stop the clicking of her needles altogether for a few seconds and sit quite still, looking at the ceiling, listening for a cry or a whimper from upstairs. But all was quiet.

"Albert," she said after a while.

"Yes, dear?"

"What was it you were going to tell me last night when you came rushing up to the bedroom? You said you had an idea for the baby."

Albert Taylor lowered the magazine on to his lap and gave her a long sly look.

"Did I?" he said.

"Yes." She waited for him to go on, but he didn't.

"What's the big joke?" she asked. "Why are you grinning like that?"

"It's a joke all right," he said.

"Tell it to me, dear."

"I'm not sure I ought to," he said. "You might call me a liar."

She had seldom seen him looking so pleased with himself as he was now, and she smiled back at him, egging him on.

"I'd just like to see your face when you hear it, Mabel, that's all."

"Albert, what *is* all this?"

He paused, refusing to be hurried.

"You do think the baby's better, don't you?" he asked.

"Of course I do."

"You agree with me that all of a sudden she's feeding marvellously and looking one-hundred-per-cent different?"

"I do, Albert, yes."

"That's good," he said, the grin widening. "You see, it's me that did it."

"Did what?"

"I cured the baby."

"Yes, dear, I'm sure you did." Mrs Taylor went right on with her knitting.

"You don't believe me, do you?"

"Of course I believe you, Albert. I give you all the credit, every bit of it."

"Then how did I do it?"

"Well," she said, pausing a moment to think. "I suppose it's simply that you're a brilliant feed-mixer. Ever since you started mixing the feeds she's got better and better."

"You mean there's some sort of an art in mixing the feeds?"

"Apparently there is." She was knitting away and smiling quietly to herself, thinking how funny men were.

"I'll tell you a secret," he said. "You're absolutely right. Although, mind you, it isn't so much *how* you mix it that counts. It's what you put in. You realize that, don't you, Mabel?"

Mrs Taylor stopped knitting and looked up sharply at her

husband. "Albert," she said, "don't tell me you've been putting things into that child's milk?"

He sat there grinning.

"Well, have you or haven't you?"

"It's possible," he said.

"I don't believe it."

He had a strange fierce way of grinning that showed his teeth.

"Albert," she said. "Stop playing with me like this."

"Yes, dear, all right."

"You haven't *really* put anything into her milk, have you? Answer me properly, Albert. This could be serious with such a tiny baby."

"The answer is yes, Mabel."

"*Albert Taylor!* How could you?"

"Now don't get excited," he said. "I'll tell you all about it if you really want me to, but for heaven's sake keep your hair on."

"It was beer!" she cried. "I just know it was beer!"

"Don't be so daft, Mabel, please."

"Then what was it?"

Albert laid his pipe down carefully on the table beside him and leaned back in his chair. "Tell me," he said, "did you ever by any chance happen to hear me mentioning something called royal jelly?"

"I did not."

"It's magic," he said. "Pure magic. And last night I suddenly got the idea that if I was to put some of this into the baby's milk . . ."

"How *dare* you!"

"Now, Mabel, you don't even know what it is yet."

"I don't care what it is," she said. "You can't go putting foreign bodies like that into a tiny baby's milk. You must be mad."

"It's perfectly harmless, Mable, otherwise I wouldn't have done it. It comes from bees."

"I might have guessed that."

"And it's so precious that pratically no one can afford to take it. When they do, it's only one little drop at a time."

"And how much did you give to our baby, might I ask?"

"Ah," he said, "that's the whole point. That's where the difference lies. I reckon that our baby, just in the last four feeds, has already swallowed about fifty times as much royal jelly as anyone else in the world has ever swallowed before. How about that?"

"Albert, stop pulling my leg."

"I swear it," he said proudly.

She sat there staring at him, her brow wrinkled, her mouth slightly open.

"You know what this stuff actually costs, Mabel, if you want to buy it? There's a place in America advertising it for sale at this very moment for something like five hundred dollars a pound jar! *Five hundred dollars!* That's more than gold, you know!"

She hadn't the faintest idea when he was talking about.

"I'll prove it," he said, and he jumped up and went across to the large bookcase where he kept all his literature about bees. On the top shelf, the back numbers of the *American Bee Journal* were neatly stacked alongside those of the *British Bee Journal*, *Beecraft*, and other magazines. He took down the last issue of the *American Bee Journal* and turned to a page of small classified advertisements at the back.

"Here you are," he said. "Exactly as I told you. 'We sell royal jelly – $480 per lb. jar wholesale.'"

He handed her the magazine so she could read it herself.

"Now do you believe me? This is an actual shop in New York, Mabel. It says so."

"It doesn't say you can go stirring it into the milk of a practically new-born baby," she said. "I don't know what's come over you, Albert, I really don't."

"It's curing her, isn't it?"

"I'm not so sure about that, now."

"Don't be so damn silly, Mabel. You know it is."

"Then why haven't other people done it with *their* babies?"

"I keep telling you," he said. "It's too expensive. Practically nobody in the world can afford to buy royal jelly just for *eating* except maybe one or two multi-millionaires. The people who buy it are the big companies that make women's face creams and things like that. They're using it as a stunt. They mix a tiny pinch of it into a big jar of face cream and it's selling like hot cakes for absolutely enormous prices. They claim it takes out the wrinkles."

"And does it?"

"Now how on earth would I know that, Mabel? Anyway,"

he said, returning to his chair, "that's not the point. The point is this. It's done so much good to our little baby just in the last few hours that I think we ought to go right on giving it to her. Now don't interrupt, Mabel. Let me finish. I've got two hundred and forty hives out there and if I turn over maybe a hundred of them to making royal jelly, we ought to be able to supply her with all she wants."

"Albert Taylor," the woman said, stretching her eyes wide and staring at him. "Have you gone out of your mind?"

"Just hear me through, will you please?"

"I forbid it," she said, "absolutely. You're not to give my baby another drop of that horrid jelly, you understand?"

"Now, Mabel . . ."

"And quite apart from that, we had a shocking honey crop last year, and if you go fooling around with those hives now, there's no telling what might not happen."

"There's nothing wrong with my hives, Mabel."

"You know very well we had only half the normal crop last year."

"Do me a favour, will you?" he said. "Let me explain some of the marvellous things this stuff does."

"You haven't even told me what it is yet."

"All right, Mabel. I'll do that too. Will you listen? Will you give me a chance to explain it?"

She sighed and picked up her knitting once more. "I suppose you might as well get it off your chest, Albert. Go on and tell me."

He paused, a bit uncertain now how to begin. It wasn't going to be easy to explain something like this to a person with no detailed knowledge of apiculture[1] at all.

"You know, don't you," he said, "that each colony has only one queen?"

"Yes."

"And that this queen lays all the eggs?"

"Yes, dear. That much I know."

"All right. Now the queen can actually lay two different kinds of eggs. You didn't know that, but she can. It's what we call one of the miracles of the hive. She can lay eggs that produce drones, and she can lay eggs that produce workers. Now if that isn't a miracle, Mabel, I don't know what is."

[1]   bee-keeping

"Yes, Albert, all right."

"The drones are the males. We don't have to worry about them. The workers are all females. So is the queen, of course. But the workers are unsexed females, if you see what I mean. Their organs are completely undeveloped, whereas the queen is tremendously sexy. She can actually lay her own weight in eggs in a single day."

He hesitated, marshalling his thoughts.

"Now what happens is this. The queen crawls around on the comb and lays her eggs in what we call cells. You know all those hundreds of little holes you see in a honeycomb? Well, a brood comb is just about the same except the cells don't have honey in them, they have eggs. She lays one egg to each cell, and in three days each of these eggs hatches out into a tiny grub. We call it a larva.

"Now, as soon as this larva appears, the nurse bees – they're young workers – all crowd round and start feeding it like mad. And you know what they feed it on?"

"Royal jelly," Mabel answered patiently.

"Right!" he cried. "That's exactly what they do feed it on. They get this stuff out of a gland in their heads and they start pumping it into the cell to feed the larva. And what happens then?"

He paused dramatically, blinking at her with his small watery-grey eyes. Then he turned slowly in his chair and reached for the magazine that he had been reading the night before.

"You want to know what happens then?" he asked, wetting his lips.

"I can hardly wait."

"'Royal jelly,'" he read aloud, "'must be a substance of tremendous nourishing power, for on this diet alone, the honey-bee larva increases in weight *fifteen hundred times* in five days!'"

"How much?"

"*Fifteen hundred times*, Mabel. And you know what that means if you put it in terms of a human being? It means," he said, lowering his voice, leaning forward, fixing her with those small pale eyes, "it means that in five days a baby weighing seven and a half pounds to start off with would increase in weight to *five tons*!"

For the second time, Mrs Taylor stopped knitting.

"Now you mustn't take that too literally, Mabel."

"Who says I mustn't?"

"It's just a scientific way of putting it, that's all."

"Very well, Albert. Go on."

"But that's only half the story," he said. "There's more to come. The really amazing thing about royal jelly, I haven't told you yet. I'm going to show you now how it can transform a plain dull-looking little worker bee with practically no sex organs at all into a great big beautiful fertile queen."

"Are you saying our baby is dull-looking and plain?" she asked sharply.

"Now don't go putting words into my mouth, Mabel, please. Just listen to this. Did you know that the queen bee and the worker bee, although they are completely different when they grow up, are both hatched out of exactly the same kind of egg?"

"I don't believe that," she said.

"It's true as I'm sitting here, Mabel, honest it is. Any time the bees want a queen to hatch out of the egg instead of a worker, they can do it."

"How?"

"Ah," he said, shaking a thick forefinger in her direction. "That's just what I'm coming to. That's the secret of the whole thing. Now – what do *you* think it is, Mabel, that makes this miracle happen?"

"Royal jelly," she answered. "You already told me."

"Royal jelly it is!" he cried, clapping his hands and bouncing up on his seat. His big round face was glowing with excitement now, and two vivid patches of scarlet had appeared high up on each cheek.

"Here's how it works. I'll put it very simply for you. The bees want a new queen. So they build an extra-large cell, a queen cell we call it, and they get the old queen to lay one of her eggs in there. The other one thousand nine hundred and ninety-nine eggs she lays in ordinary worker cells. Now. As soon as these eggs hatch into larvae, the nurse bees rally round and start pumping in the royal jelly. All of them get it, workers as well as queen. But here's the vital thing, Mabel, so listen carefully. Here's where the difference comes. The worker larvae only receive the special marvellous food for the *first three days* of their larval life. After that they have a complete change of diet. What really happens is they get weaned, except that it's not like an ordinary weaning because it's so sudden. After the third day they're put straight away on to more or less routine bees' food – a mixture of honey and pollen – and then about two weeks later they emerge from the cells as workers.

"But not so the larva in the queen cell! This one gets royal jelly *all the way through its larval life*. The nurse bees simply pour it into the cell, so much so in fact that the little larva is literally floating in it. And that's what makes it into a queen!"

"You can't prove it," she said.

"Don't talk so damn silly, Mabel, please. Thousands of people have proved it time and time again, famous scientists in every country in the world. All you have to do is take a larva out of a worker cell and put it in a queen cell – that's what we call grafting – and just so long as the nurse bees keep it well supplied with royal jelly, then presto! – it'll grow up into a queen! And what makes it more marvellous still is the absolutely enormous difference between a queen and a worker when they grow up. The abdomen is a different shape. The sting is different. The legs are different. The . . ."

"In what way are the legs different?" she asked, testing him.

"The legs? Well, the workers have little pollen baskets on their legs for carrying the pollen. The queen has none. Now here's another thing. The queen has fully developed sex organs. The workers don't. And most amazing of all, Mabel, the queen lives for an average of four to six years. The worker hardly lives that many months. And all this difference simply because one of them got royal jelly and the other didn't!"

"It's pretty hard to believe," she said, "that a food can do all that."

"Of course it's hard to believe. It's another of the miracles of the hive. In fact it's the biggest ruddy miracle of them all. It's such a hell of a big miracle that it's baffled the greatest men of science for hundreds of years. Wait a moment. Stay there. Don't move."

Again he jumped up and went over to the bookcase and started rummaging among the books and magazines.

"I'm going to find you a few of the reports. Here we are. Here's one of them. Listen to this." He started reading aloud from a copy of the *American Bee Journal*:

"'Living in Toronto at the head of a fine research laboratory given to him by the people of Canada in recognition of his truly great contribution to humanity in the discovery of insulin, Dr Frederick A. Banting became curious about royal jelly. He requested his staff to do a basic fractional analysis. . .'"

He paused.

"Well, there's no need to read it all, but here's what happened. Dr Banting and his people took some royal jelly from queen cells that contained two-day-old larvae, and then they started analysing it. And what d'you think they found?

"They found," he said, "that royal jelly contained phenols, sterols, glycerils, dextrose, *and* – now here it comes – and eighty to eighty-five per cent *unidentified* acids!"

He stood beside the bookcase with the magazine in his hand, smiling a funny little furtive smile of triumph, and his wife watched him, bewildered.

He was not a tall man; he had a thick plump pulpy-looking body that was built close to the ground on abbreviated legs. The legs were slightly bowed. The head was huge and round, covered with bristly short-cut hair, and the greater part of the face – now that he had given up shaving altogether – was hidden by a brownish yellow fuzz about an inch long. In one way and another, he was rather grotesque to look at, there was no denying that.

"Eighty to eighty-five per cent," he said, "unidentified acids. Isn't that fantastic?" He turned back to the bookshelf and began hunting through the other magazines.

"What does it mean, unidentified acids?"

"That's the whole point! No one knows! Not even Banting could find out. You've heard of Banting?"

"No."

"He just happens to be about the most famous living doctor in the world today, that's all."

Looking at him now as he buzzed around in front of the bookcase with his bristly head and his hairy face and his plump pulpy body, she couldn't help thinking that somehow, in some curious way, there was a touch of the bee about this man. She had often seen women grow to look like the horses that they rode, and she had noticed that people who bred birds or bull terriers or pomeranians frequently resembled in some small but startling manner the creature of their choice. But up until now it had never occurred to her that her husband might look like a bee. It shocked her a bit.

"And did Banting ever try to eat it," she asked, "this royal jelly?"

"Of course he didn't eat it, Mabel. He didn't have enough for that. It's too precious."

"You know something?" she said, staring at him but smiling a little all the same. "You're getting to look just a teeny bit like a bee yourself, did you know that?"

He turned and looked at her.

"I suppose it's the beard mostly," she said. "I do wish you'd stop wearing it. Even the colour is sort of bee-ish, don't you think?"

"What the hell are you talking about, Mabel?"

"Albert," she said. "Your language."

"Do you want to hear any more of this or don't you?"

"Yes, dear, I'm sorry. I was only joking. Do go on."

He turn away again and pulled another magazine out of the bookcase and began leafing through the pages. "Now just listen to this, Mabel. 'In 1939, Heyl experimented with twenty-one-day-old rats, injecting them with royal jelly in varying amounts. As a result, he found a precocious follicular[1] development of the ovaries directly in proportion to the quantity of royal jelly injected.'"

"There!" she cried. "I knew it!"

"Knew what?"

"I knew something terrible would happen."

"Nonsense. There's nothing wrong with that. Now here's another, Mabel. 'Still and Burdett found that a male rat which hitherto had been unable to breed, upon receiving a minute daily dose of royal jelly, became a father many times over.'"

"Albert," she cried, "this stuff is *much* too strong to give to a baby! I don't like it at all."

"Nonsense, Mabel."

"Then why do they only try it out on rats, tell me that? Why don't some of these famous scientists take it themselves? They're too clever, that's why. Do you think Dr Banting is going to risk finishing up with precious ovaries? Not him."

"But they *have* given it to people, Mabel. Here's a whole article about it. Listen." He turned the page and again began reading from the magazine. "'In Mexico, in 1953, a group of

---

[1] sac containing hair root

enlightened physicians began prescribing minute doses of royal jelly for such things as cerebral neuritis, arthritis, diabetes, autointoxication from tobacco, impotence in men, asthma, croup and gout. . . There are stacks of signed testimonials. . . A celebrated stockbroker in Mexico City contracted a particularly stubborn case of psoriasis. He became physically unattractive. His clients began to forsake him. His business began to suffer. In desperation he turned to royal jelly – one drop with every meal – and presto! – he was cured in a fortnight. A waiter in the Café Jena, also in Mexico City, reported that his father, after taking minute doses of this wonder substance in capsule form, sired a healthy boy child at the age of ninety. A bullfight promoter in Acapulco, finding himself landed with a rather lethargic-looking bull, injected it with one gramme of royal jelly (an excessive dose) just before it entered the arena. Thereupon, the beast became so swift and savage that it promptly dispatched two picadors, three horses, and a matador, and finally . . .'"

"Listen!" Mrs Taylor said, interrupting him. "I think the baby's crying."

Albert glanced up from his reading. Sure enough, a lusty yelling noise was coming from the bedroom above.

"She must be hungry," he said.

His wife looked at the clock. "Good gracious me!" she cried, jumping up. "It's past her time again already! You mix the feed, Albert, quickly, while I bring her down! But hurry! I don't want to keep her waiting."

In half a minute, Mrs Taylor was back, carrying the screaming infant in her arms. She was flustered now, still quite unaccustomed to the ghastly nonstop racket that a healthy baby makes when it wants its food. "Do be quick, Albert!" she called, settling herself in the armchair and arranging the child on her lap. "Please hurry!"

Albert entered from the kitchen and handed her the bottle of warm milk. "It's just right," he said. "You don't have to test it."

She hitched the baby's head a little higher in the crook of her arm, then pushed the rubber teat straight into the wide-open yelling mouth. The baby grabbed the teat and began to suck. The yelling stopped. Mrs Taylor relaxed.

"Oh, Albert, isn't she lovely?"

"She's terrific, Mabel – thanks to royal jelly."

"Now, dear, I don't want to hear another word about that nasty stuff. It frightens me to death."

"You're making a big mistake," he said.

"We'll see about that."

The baby went on sucking the bottle.

"I do believe she's going to finish the whole lot again, Albert."

"I'm sure she is," he said.

And a few minutes later, the milk was all gone.

"Oh, what a good girl you are!" Mrs Taylor cried, as very gently she started to withdraw the nipple. The baby sensed what she was doing and sucked harder, trying to hold on. The woman gave a quick little tug, and *plop*, out it came.

"Waa! Waa! Waa! Waa!" the baby yelled.

"Nasty old wind," Mrs Taylor said, hoisting the child on to her shoulder and patting its back.

It belched twice in quick succession.

"There you are, my darling, you'll be all right now."

For a few seconds, the yelling stopped. Then it started again.

"Keep belching her," Albert said. "She's drunk it too quickly."

His wife lifted the baby back on to her shoulder. She rubbed its spine. She changed it from one shoulder to the other. She lay it on its stomach on her lap. She sat it up on her knee. But it didn't belch again, and the yelling became louder and more insistent every minute.

"Good for the lungs," Albert Taylor said, grinning. "That's the way they exercise their lungs, Mabel, did you know what?"

"There, there, there," the wife said, kissing it all over the face. "There, there, there."

They waited another five minutes, but not for one moment did the screaming stop.

"Change the nappy," Albert said. "It's got a wet nappy, that's all it is." He fetched a clean one from the kitchen, and Mrs Taylor took the old one off and put the new one on.

This made no difference at all.

"Waa! Waa! Waa! Waa! Waa!" the baby yelled.

"You didn't stick the safety pin through the skin, did you, Mabel?"

"Of course I didn't," she said, feeling under the nappy with her fingers to make sure.

The parents sat opposite one another in their armchairs,

smiling nervously, watching the baby on the mother's lap, waiting for it to tire and stop screaming.

"You know what?" Albert Taylor said at last.

"What?"

"I'll bet she's still hungry. I'll bet all she wants is another swig at that bottle. How about me fetching her an extra lot?"

"I don't think we ought to do that, Albert."

"It'll do her good," he said, getting up from his chair. "I'm going to warm her up a second helping."

He went into the kitchen, and was away several minutes. When he returned he was holding a bottle brimful of milk.

"I made her a double," he announced. "Eight ounces. Just in case."

"Albert! Are you mad? Don't you know it's just as bad to overfeed as it is to underfeed?"

"You don't have to give her the lot, Mabel. You can stop any time you like. Go on," he said, standing over her. "Give her a drink."

Mrs Taylor began to tease the baby's upper lip with the end of the nipple. The tiny mouth closed like a trap over the rubber teat and suddenly there was silence in the room. The baby's whole body relaxed and a look of absolute bliss came over its face as it started to drink.

"There you are, Mabel! What did I tell you?"

The woman didn't answer.

"She's ravenous, that's what she is. Just look at her suck."

Mrs Taylor was watching the level of the milk in the bottle. It was dropping fast, and before long three or four ounces out of the eight had disappeared.

"There," she said. "That'll do."

"You can't pull it away now, Mabel."

"Yes, dear. I must."

"Go on, woman. Give her the rest and stop fussing."

"But *Albert* . . ."

"She's famished, can't you see that? Go on, my beauty," he said. "You finish that bottle."

"I don't like it, Albert," the wife said, but she didn't pull the bottle away.

"She's making up for lost time, Mabel, that's all she's doing."

Five minutes later the bottle was empty. Slowly, Mrs Taylor

withdrew the nipple, and this time there was no protest from the baby, no sound at all. It lay peacefully on the mother's lap, the eyes glazed with contentment, the mouth half-open, the lips smeared with milk.

"Twelve whole ounces, Mabel!" Albert Taylor said. "Three times the normal amount! Isn't that amazing.

The woman was staring down at the baby. And now the old anxious tight-lipped look of the frightened mother was slowly returning to her face.

"What's the matter with *you*?" Albert asked. "You're not worried by that, are you? You can't expect her to get back to normal on a lousy four ounces, don't be ridiculous."

"Come here, Albert," she said.

"What?"

"I said come here."

He went over and stood beside her.

"Take a good look and tell me if you see anything different."

He peered closely at the baby. "She seems bigger, Mabel, if that's what you mean. Bigger and fatter."

"Hold her," she ordered. "Go on, pick her up."

He reached out and lifted the baby up off the mother's lap. "Good God!" he cried. "She weighs a ton!"

"Exactly."

"Now isn't that marvellous!" he cried, beaming. "I'll bet she must be back to normal already!"

"It frightens me, Albert. It's too quick."

"Nonsense, woman."

"It's that digusting jelly that's done it," she said. "I hate the stuff."

"There's nothing disgusting about royal jelly," he answered, indignant.

"Don't be a fool, Albert! You think it's *normal* for a child to start putting on weight at this speed?"

"You're never satisfied!" he cried. "You're scared stiff when she's losing and now you're absolutely terrified because she's gaining! What's the matter with you, Mabel?"

The woman got up from her chair with the baby in her arms and started towards the door. "All I can say is," she said, "it's lucky I'm here to see you don't give her any more of it, that's all I can say." She went out, and Albert watched her through the open door as she crossed the hall to the foot of the stairs and started to ascend, and when she reached the third or fourth step she suddenly stopped and stood quite still for several seconds as though remembering something. Then she turned and came down again rather quickly and re-entered the room.

"Albert," she said.

"Yes?"

"I assume there wasn't any royal jelly in this last feed we've just given her?"

"I don't see why you should assume that, Mabel."

"Albert!"

"What's wrong?" he asked, soft and innocent.

"How *dare* you!" she cried.

Albert Taylor's great bearded face took on a pained and puzzled look. "I think you ought to be very glad she's got another big dose of it inside her," he said. "Honest I do. And this *is* a big dose, Mabel, believe you me."

The woman was standing just inside the doorway clasping the sleeping baby in her arms and staring at her husband with huge eyes. She stood very erect, her body absolutely stiff with fury, her face paler, more tight-lipped than ever.

"You mark my works," Albert was saying, "you're going to have a nipper there soon that'll win first prize in any baby show in the *entire* country. Hey, why don't you weigh her now and see what she is? You want me to get the scales, Mabel, so you can weigh her?"

The woman walked straight over to the large table in the centre of the room and laid the baby down and quickly started taking off its clothes. "Yes!" she snapped. "Get the scales!" Off came the little nightgown, then the undervest.

Then she unpinned the nappy and she drew it away and the baby lay naked on the table.

"But Mabel!" Albert cried. "It's a miracle! She's fat as a puppy!"

Indeed, the amount of flesh the child had put on since the day before was astounding. The small sunken chest with the rib bones showing all over it was now plump and round as a barrel, and the belly was bulging high in the air. Curiously, though, the arms and legs did not seem to have grown in proportion. Still short and skinny, they looked like little sticks protruding from a ball of fat.

"Look!" Albert said. "She's even beginning to get a bit of fuzz on the tummy to keep her warm!" He put out a hand and was about to run the tips of his fingers over the powdering of silky yellowy-brown hairs that had suddenly appeared on the baby's stomach.

"*Don't you touch her!*" the woman cried. She turned and faced him, her eyes blazing, and she looked suddenly like some kind of little fighting bird with her neck arched over towards him as though she were about to fly at his face and peck his eyes out.

"Now wait a minute," he said, retreating.

"You must be mad!" she cried.

"Now wait just one minute, Mabel, will you please, because if you're still thinking this stuff is dangerous. . . That *is* what you're thinking, isn't it? All right, then. Listen carefully. I shall now proceed to *prove* to you once and for all, Mabel, that royal jelly is absolutely harmless to human beings, even in enormous doses. For example – why do you think we had only half the usual honey crop last summer? Tell me that."

His retreat, walking backwards, had taken him three or four yards away from her, where he seemed to feel more comfortable.

"The reason we had only half the usual crop last summer," he said slowly, lowering his voice, "was because I turned one hundred of my hives over to the production of royal jelly."

"You *what*?"

"Ah," he whispered. "I thought that might surprise you a bit. And I've been making it ever since right under your very nose." His small eyes were glinting at her, and a slow sly smile was creeping around the corners of his mouth.

"You'll never guess the reason, either," he said. "I've been afraid to mention it up to now because I thought it might . . . well . . . sort of embarrass you."

There was a slight pause. He had his hands clasped high in front of him, level with his chest, and he was rubbing one palm against the other, making a soft scraping noise.

"You remember that bit I read you out of the magazine? That bit about the rat? Let me see now, how does it go? 'Still and Burdett found that a male rat which hitherto had been unable to breed . . .'" He hesitated, the grin widening, showing his teeth.

"You get the message, Mabel?"

She stood quite still, facing him.

"The very first time I ever read that sentence, Mabel, I

jumped straight out of my chair and I said to myself if it'll work with a lousy rat, I said, then there's no reason on earth why it shouldn't work with Albert Taylor."

He paused again, craning his head forward and turning one ear slightly in his wife's direction, waiting for her to say something. But she didn't.

"And here's another thing," he went on. "It made me feel so absolutely marvellous, Mabel, and so sort of completely different to what I was before that I went right on taking it even after you'd announced the joyful tidings. *Buckets* of it I must have swallowed during the last twelve months."

The big heavy haunted-looking eyes of the woman were moving intently over the man's face and neck. There was no skin showing at all on the neck, not even at the side below the ears. The whole of it, to a point where it disappeared into the collar of the shirt, was covered all the way around with those shortish silky hairs, yellowy black.

"Mind you," he said, turning away from her, gazing lovingly now at the baby, "it's going to work far better on a tiny infant than on a fully developed man like me. You've only got to look at her to see that, don't you agree?"

The woman's eyes travelled slowly downward and settled on the baby. The baby was lying naked on the table, fat and white and comatose, like some gigantic grub that was approaching the end of its larval life and would soon emerge into the world complete with mandibles and wings.

"Why don't you cover her up, Mabel?" he said. "We don't want our little queen to catch a cold."

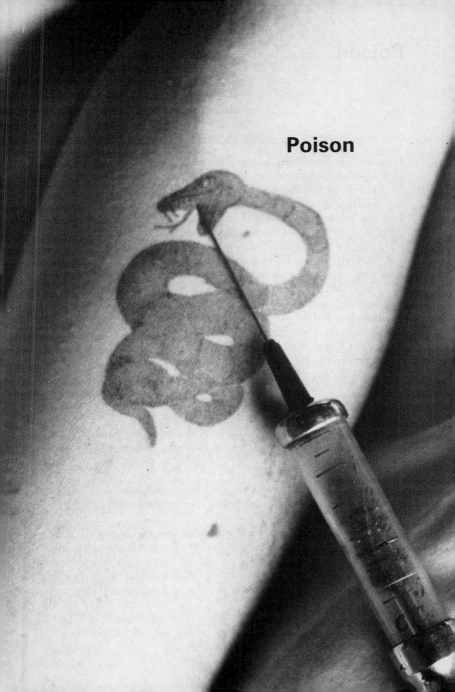

Poison

Poison

It must have been around midnight when I drove home, and as I approached the gates of the bungalow I switched off the headlamps of the car so the beam wouldn't swing in through the window of the side bedroom and wake Harry Pope. But I needn't have bothered. Coming up the drive I noticed his light was still on, so he was awake anyway – unless perhaps he'd dropped off while reading.

I parked the car and went up the five steps to the balcony, counting each step carefully in the dark so I wouldn't take an extra one which wasn't there when I got to the top. I crossed the balcony, pushed through the screen doors into the house itself and switched on the light in the hall. I went across to the door of Harry's room, opened it quietly, and looked in.

He was lying on the bed and I could see he was awake. But he didn't move. He didn't even turn his head towards me, but I heard him say, "Timber, Timber, come here."

He spoke slowly, whispering each word carefully, separately, and I pushed the door right open and started to go quickly across the room.

"Stop. Wait a moment, Timber." I could hardly hear what he was saying. He seemed to be straining enormously to get the words out.

"What's the matter, Harry?"

"Sshhh!" he whispered. "Sshhh! For God's sake don't make a noise. Take your shoes off before you come nearer. *Please* do as I say, Timber."

The way he was speaking reminded me of George Barling after he got shot in the stomach when he stood leaning against a crate containing a spare aeroplane engine, holding both hands on his stomach and saying things about the German pilot in just the same hoarse straining half whisper Harry was using now.

"Quickly, Timber, but take your shoes off first."

I couldn't understand about taking off the shoes but I

figured that if he was as ill as he sounded I'd better humour him, so I bent down and removed the shoes and left them in the middle of the floor. Then I went over to his bed.

"Don't touch the bed! For God's sake don't touch the bed!" He was still speaking like he'd been shot in the stomach and I could see him lying there on his back with a single sheet covering three-quarters of his body. He was wearing a pair of pyjamas with blue, brown, and white stripes, and he was sweating terribly. It was a hot night and I was sweating a little myself, but not like Harry. His whole face was wet and the pillow around his head was sodden with moisture. It looked like a bad go of malaria to me.

"What is it, Harry?"

"A krait," he said.

"A *krait*! Oh, my God! Where'd it bite you? How long ago?"

"Shut up," he whispered.

"Listen, Harry," I said, and I leaned forward and touched his shoulder. "We've got to be quick. Come on now, quickly, tell me where it bit you." He was lying there very still and tense as though he was holding on to himself hard because of sharp pain.

"I haven't been bitten," he whispered. "Not yet. It's on my stomach. Lying there asleep."

I took a quick pace backwards. I couldn't help it, and I stared at his stomach or rather at the sheet that covered it. The sheet was rumpled in several places and it was impossible to tell if there was anything underneath.

You don't really mean there's a krait lying on your stomach now?"

"I swear it."

"How did it get there?" I shouldn't have asked the question because it was easy to see he wasn't fooling. I should have told him to keep quiet.

"I was reading," Harry said, and he spoke very slowly, taking each word in turn and speaking it carefully so as not to move the muscles of his stomach. "Lying on my back reading and I felt something on my chest, behind the book. Sort of tickling. Then out of the corner of my eye saw this little krait sliding over my pyjamas. Small, about ten inches. Knew I mustn't move. Couldn't have anyway. Lay there watching it. Thought it would go over top of the sheet," Harry paused and was silent for a few moments. His eyes looked down along

117

his body towards the place where the sheet covered his stomach, and I could see he was watching to make sure his whispering wasn't disturbing the thing that lay there.

"There was a fold in the sheet," he said, speaking more slowly than ever now and so softly I had to lean close to hear him. "See it, it's still there. It went under that. I could feel it through my pyjamas, moving on my stomach. Then it stopped moving and now it's lying there in the warmth. Probably asleep. I've been waiting for you." He raised his eyes and looked at me.

"How long ago?"

"Hours," he whispered. "Hours and bloody hours and hours, I can't keep still much longer. I've been wanting to cough."

There was not much doubt about the truth of Harry's story. As a matter of fact it wasn't a surprising thing for a krait to do. They hang around people's houses and they go for the warm places. The surprising thing was that Harry hadn't been bitten. The bite is quite deadly except sometimes when you catch it at once and they kill a fair number of people each year in Bengal, mostly in the villages.

"All right, Harry," I said, and now I was whispering too. "Don't move and don't talk any more unless you have to. You know it won't bite unless it's frightened. We'll fix it in no time."

I went softly out of the room in my stocking feet and fetched a small sharp knife from the kitchen. I put it in my trouser pocket ready to use instantly in case something went wrong while we were still thinking out a plan. If Harry coughed or moved or did something to frighten the krait and got bitten, I was going to be ready to cut the bitten place and try to suck the venom out. I came back to the bedroom and Harry was still lying there very quiet and sweating all over his face. His eyes followed me as I moved across the room to his bed and I could see he was wondering what I'd been up to. I stood beside him, trying to think of the best thing to do.

"Harry," I said, and now when I spoke I put my mouth almost on his ear so I wouldn't have to raise my voice above the softest whisper, "I think the best thing to do is for me to draw the sheet back very, very gently. Then we could have a look first. I think I could do that without disturbing it."

"Don't be a damn fool." There was no expression in his

voice. He spoke each word too slowly, too carefully, and too softly for that. The expression was in the eyes and around the corners of the mouth.

"Why not?"

"The light would frighten him. It's dark under there now."

"Then how about whipping the sheet back quick and brushing it off before it has time to strike?"

"Why don't you get a doctor?" Harry said. The way he looked at me told me I should have thought of that myself in the first place.

"A doctor. Of course. That's it. I'll get Ganderbai."

I tiptoed out to the hall, looked up Ganderbai's number in the book, lifted the phone and told the operator to hurry.

"Dr Ganderbai," I said. "This is Timber Woods."

"Hello, Mr Woods. You not in bed yet?"

"Look, could you come round at once? And bring serum[1] – for a krait bite."

"Who's been bitten?" The question came so sharply it was like a small explosion in my ear.

"No one. No one yet. But Harry Pope's in bed and he's got one lying on his stomach – asleep under the sheet on his stomach."

For about three seconds there was silence on the line. Then speaking slowly, not like an explosion now but slowly, precisely, Ganderbai said, "Tell him to keep quite still. He is not to move or to talk. Do you understand?"

"Of course."

"I'll come at once!" He rang off and I went back to the bedroom. Harry's eyes watched me as I walked across to his bed.

"Ganderbai's coming. He said for you to lie still."

"What in God's name does he think I'm doing!"

"Look, Harry, he said no talking. Absolutely no talking. Either of us."

"Why don't you shut up then?" When he said this, one side of his mouth started twitching with rapid little downward movements that continued for a while after he finished speaking. I took out my handkerchief and very gently I wiped the sweat off his face and neck, and I could feel the slight

---

[1] liquid in the blood which can be injected into body to fight disease

twitching of the muscle – the one he used for smiling – as my fingers passed over it with the handkerchief.

I slipped out to the kitchen, got some ice from the ice-box, rolled it up in a napkin, and began to crush it small. That business of the mouth, I didn't like that. Or the way he talked, either. I carried the ice pack back to the bedroom and laid it across Harry's forehead.

"Keep you cool."

He screwed up his eyes and drew breath sharply through his teeth. "Take it away," he whispered. "Make me cough." His smiling-muscle began to twitch again.

The beam of a headlamp shone through the window as Ganderbai's car swung around to the front of the bungalow. I went out to meet him, holding the ice pack with both hands.

"How is it?" Ganderbai asked, but he didn't stop to talk; he walked on past me across the balcony and through the screen doors into the hall. "Where is he? Which room?"

He put his bag down on a chair in the hall and followed me into Harry's room. He was wearing soft-soled bedroom slippers and he walked across the floor noiselessly, delicately, like a cat. Harry watched him out of the sides of his eyes. When Ganderbai reached the bed he looked down at Harry and smiled, confident and reassuring, nodding his head to tell Harry it was a simple matter and he was not to worry but just to leave it to Dr Ganderbai. Then he turned and went back to the hall and I followed him.

"First thing is to try to get some serum into him," he said, and he opened his bag and started to make preparations. "Intravenously[1]. But I must do it neatly. Don't want to make him flinch."

We went into the kitchen and he sterilized a needle. He had a hypodermic[2] syringe in one hand and a small bottle in the other and he stuck the needle through the rubber top of the bottle and began drawing a pale yellow liquid up into the syringe by pulling out the plunger. Then he handed the syringe to me.

"Hold that till I ask for it."

He picked up the bag and together we returned to the room. Harry's eyes were bright now and wide open. Ganderbai bent

---

[1] into a vein
[2] for injection beneath the skin

over Harry and very cautiously, like a man handling sixteenth-century lace, he rolled up the pyjama sleeve to the elbow without moving the arm. I noticed he stood well away from the bed.

He whispered, "I'm going to give you an injection. Serum. Just a prick but try not to move. Don't tighten your stomach muscles. Let them go limp."

Harry looked at the syringe.

Ganderbai took a piece of red rubber tubing from his bag and slid one end under and up and around Harry's biceps; then he tied the tubing tight with a knot. He sponged a small area of the bare forearm with alcohol, handed the swab to me and took the syringe from my hand. He held it up to the light, squinting at the calibrations, squirting out some of the yellow fluid. I stood still beside him, watching. Harry was watching too and sweating all over his face so it shone like it was smeared thick with face cream melting on his skin and running down on to the pillow.

I could see the blue vein on the inside of Harry's forearm, swollen now because of the tourniquet,[1] and then I saw the needle above the vein, Ganderbai holding the syringe almost flat against the arm, sliding the needle in sideways through the skin into the blue vein, sliding it slowly but so firmly it went in smooth as into cheese. Harry looked at the ceiling and closed his eyes and opened them again, but he didn't move.

When it was finished Ganderbai leaned forward putting his mouth close to Harry's ear. "Now you'll be all right even if you *are* bitten. But don't move. Please don't move. I'll be back in a moment.

He picked up his bag and went out to the hall and I followed.

"Is he safe now?" I asked.

"No."

"How safe is he?"

The little Indian doctor stood there in the hall rubbing his lower lip.

"It must give some protection, mustn't it?" I asked.

He turned away and walked to the screen doors that led on to the verandah. I thought he was going through them, but

---

[1] bandage for stopping flow of blood through artery

he stopped this side of the doors and stood looking out into the night.

"Isn't the serum very good?" I asked.

"Unfortunately not," he answered without turning round. "It might save him. It might not. I am trying to think of something else to do."

"Shall we draw the sheet back quick and brush it off before it has time to strike?"

"Never! We are not entitled to take a risk." He spoke sharply and his voice was pitched a little higher than usual.

"We can't very well leave him lying there," I said. "He's getting nervous."

"Please! Please!" he said, turning round, holding both hands up in the air. "Not so fast, please. This is not a matter to rush into baldheaded." He wiped his forehead with his handkerchief and stood there, frowning, nibbling his lip.

"You see," he said at last. "There is a way to do this. You know what we must do − we must administer an anaesthetic to the creature where it lies."

It was a splendid idea.

"It is not safe," he continued, "because a snake is cold-blooded and anaesthetic does not work so well or so quick with such animals, but it is better than any other thing to do. We could use ether . . . chloroform . . ." He was speaking slowly and trying to think the thing out while he talked.

"Which shall we use?"

"Chloroform," he said suddenly "Ordinary chloroform. That is best. Now quick!" He took my arm and pulled me towards the balcony. "Drive to my house! By the time you get there I will have waked up my boy on the telephone and he will show you my poisons cupboard. Here is the key of the cupboard. Take a bottle of chloroform. It has an orange label and the name is printed on it. I stay here in case anything happens. Be quick now, hurry! No, no, you don't need your shoes!"

I drove fast and in about fifteen minutes I was back with the bottle of chloroform. Ganderbai came out of Harry's room and met me in the hall. "You got it?" he said. "Good, good. I just been telling him what we are going to do. But now we must hurry. It is not easy for him in there like that all this time. I am afraid he might move."

He went back to the bedroom and I followed, carrying the

bottle carefully with both hands. Harry was lying on the bed in precisely the same position as before with the sweat pouring down his cheeks. His face was white and wet. He turned his eyes towards me and I smiled at him and nodded confidently. He continued to look at me. I raised my thumb, giving him the okay signal. He closed his eyes. Ganderbai was squatting down by the bed, and on the floor beside him was the hollow rubber tube that he had previously used as a tourniquet and he'd got a small paper funnel fitted into one end of the tube.

He began to pull a little piece of the sheet out from under the mattress. He was working directly in line with Harry's stomach, about eighteen inches from it, and I watched his fingers as they tugged gently at the edge of the sheet. He worked so slowly it was almost impossible to discern any movement either in his fingers or in the sheet that was being pulled.

Finally he succeeded in making an opening under the sheet and he took the rubber tube and inserted one end of it in the opening so that it would slide under the sheet along the mattress towards Harry's body. I do not know how long it took him to slide that tube in a few inches. It may have been twenty minutes, it may have been forty. I never once saw the tube move. I knew it was going in because the visible part of it grew gradually shorter, but I doubted that the krait could have felt even the faintest vibration. Ganderbai himself was sweating now, large pearls of sweat standing out all over his forehead and along his upper lip. But his hands were steady and I noticed that his eyes were watching, not the tube in his hands, but the area of crumpled sheet above Harry's stomach.

Without looking up, he held out a hand to me for the chloroform. I twisted out the ground-glass stopper and put the bottle right into his hand, not letting go till I was sure he had a good hold on it. Then he jerked his head for me to come closer and he whispered, "Tell him I'm going to soak the mattress and that it will be very cold under his body. He must be ready for that and he must not move. Tell him now."

I bent over Harry and passed on the message.

"Why doesn't he get on with it?" Harry said.

"He's going to now, Harry. But it'll feel very cold, so be ready for it."

"Oh, God Almighty, get on, get on!" For the first time he

raised his voice, and Ganderbai glanced up sharply, watched him for a few seconds, then went back to his business.

Ganderbai poured a few drops of chloroform into the paper funnel and waited while it ran down the tube. Then he poured some more. Then he waited again, and the heavy sickening smell of chloroform spread out over the room bringing with it faint unpleasant memories of white-coated nurses and white surgeons standing in a white room around a long white table. Ganderbai was pouring steadily now and I could see the heavy vapour of the chloroform swirling slowly like smoke above the paper funnel. He paused, held the bottle up to the light, poured one more funnelful and handed the bottle back to me. Slowly he drew out the rubber tube from under the sheet; then he stood up.

The strain of inserting the tube and pouring the chloroform must have been great, and I recollect that when Ganderbai turned and whispered to me, his voice was small and tired. "We'll give it fifteen minutes. Just to be safe."

I leaned over to tell Harry. "We're going to give it fifteen minutes, just to be safe. But it's probably done for already."

"Then why for God's sake don't you look and see!" Again he spoke loudly and Ganderbai sprang round, his small brown face suddenly very angry. He had almost pure black eyes and he stared at Harry and Harry's smiling-muscle started to twitch. I took my handkerchief and wiped his wet face, trying to stroke his forehead a little for comfort as I did so.

Then we stood and waited beside the bed, Ganderbai watching Harry's face all the time in a curious intense manner. The little Indian was concentrating all his will power on keeping Harry quiet. He never once took his eyes from the patient and although he made no sound, he seemed somehow to be shouting at him all the time, saying: Now listen, you've got to listen, you're not going to go spoiling this now, d'you hear me; and Harry lay there twitching his mouth, sweating, closing his eyes, opening them, looking at me, at the sheet, at the ceiling, at me again, but never at Ganderbai. Yet somehow Ganderbai was holding him. The smell of chloroform was oppressive and it made me feel sick, but I couldn't leave the room now. I had the feeling someone was blowing up a huge balloon and I could see it was going to bust, but I couldn't look away.

At length Ganderbai turned and nodded and I knew he was

ready to proceed. "You go over to the other side of the bed," he said. "We will each take one side of sheet and draw it back together, but very slowly, please, and very quietly."

"Keep still now, Harry," I said and I went around to the other side of the bed and took hold of the sheet. Ganderbai stood opposite me, and together we began to draw back the sheet, lifting it up clear of Harry's body, taking it back very slowly, both of us standing well away but at the same time bending forward, trying to peer underneath it. The smell of chloroform was awful. I remember trying to hold my breath and when I couldn't do that any longer I tried to breathe shallow so the stuff wouldn't get into my lungs.

The whole of Harry's chest was visible now, or rather the striped pyjama top which covered it, and then I saw the white cord of his pyjama trousers, neatly tied in a bow. A little farther and I saw a button, a mother-of-pearl button, and that was something I had never had on my pyjamas, a fly button, let alone a mother-of-pearl one. This Harry, I thought, he is very refined. It is odd how one sometimes has frivolous[1] thoughts at exciting moments, and I distinctly remember thinking about Harry being very refined when I saw that button.

Apart from the button there was nothing on his stomach.

We pulled the sheet back faster then, and when we had uncovered his legs and feet we let the sheet drop over the end of the bed on to the floor.

"Don't move," Ganderbai said, "don't move, Mr Pope"; and he began to peer around along the side of Harry's body and under his legs.

"We must be careful," he said. "It may be anywhere. It could be up the leg of his pyjamas."

When Ganderbai said this, Harry quickly raised his head from the pillow and looked down at his legs. It was the first time he had moved. Then suddenly he jumped up, stood on his bed and shook his legs one after the other violently in the air. At that moment we both thought he had been bitten and Ganderbai was already reaching down into his bag for a scalpel and a tourniquet when Harry ceased his caperings and stood still and looked at the mattress he was standing on and shouted, "It's not there!"

---

[1] silly, lacking seriousness

Ganderbai straightened up and for a moment he too looked at the mattress; then he looked up at Harry. Harry was all right. He hadn't been bitten and now he wasn't going to get bitten and he wasn't going to be killed and everything was fine. But that didn't seem to make anyone feel any better.

"Mr Pope, you are of course *quite* sure you saw it in the first place?" There was a note of sarcasm in Ganderbai's voice that he would never have employed in ordinary circumstances. "You don't think you might possibly have been dreaming, do you, Mr Pope?" The way Ganderbai was looking at Harry, I realized that the sarcasm was not seriously intended. He was only easing up a bit after the strain.

Harry stood on his bed in his striped pyjamas, glaring at Ganderbai, and the colour began to spread out over his cheeks.

"Are you telling me I'm a liar?" he shouted.

Ganderbai remained absolutely still, watching Harry. Harry took a pace forward on the bed and there was a shining look in his eyes.

"Why, you dirty little Hindu sewer rat!"

"Shut up, Harry!" I said.

"You dirty black —"

"Harry!" I called. "Shut up, Harry!" It was terrible, the things he was saying.

Ganderbai went out of the room as though neither of us was there and I followed him and put my arm around his shoulder as he walked across the hall and out on to the balcony.

"Don't you listen to Harry," I said. "This thing's made him so he doesn't know what he's saying."

We went down the steps from the balcony to the drive and across the drive in the darkness to where his old Morris car was parked. He opened the door and got in.

"You did a wonderful job," I said. "Thank you so very much for coming."

"All he needs is a good holiday," he said quietly, without looking at me, then he started the engine and drove off.

A Piece of Cake

A Piece of Cake
My first story – 1942

I do not remember much of it; not beforehand anyway; not until it happened.

There was the landing at Fouka, where the Blenheim boys were helpful and gave us tea while we were being refuelled. I remember the quietness of the Blenheim boys, how they came into the mess-tent to get some tea and sat down to drink it without saying anything; how they got up and went out when they had finished drinking and still they did not say anything. And I knew that each one was holding himself together because the going was not very good right then. They were having to go out too often, and there were no replacements coming along.

We thanked them for the tea and went out to see if they had finished refuelling our Gladiators. I remember that there was a wind blowing which made the windsock stand out straight, like a signpost, and the sand was blowing up around our legs and making a rustling noise as it swished against the tents, and the tents flapped in the wind so that they were like canvas men clapping their hands.

"Bomber boys unhappy," Peter said.

"Not unhappy," I answered.

"Well, they're browned off."

"No. They've had it, that's all. But they'll keep going. You can see they're trying to keep going."

Our two old Gladiators were standing beside each other in the sand and the airmen in their khaki shirts and shorts seemed still to be busy with refuelling. I was wearing a thin white cotton flying suit and Peter had on a blue one. It wasn't necessary to fly with anything warmer.

Peter said, "How far away is it?"

"Twenty-one miles beyond Charing Cross," I answered, "on the right side of the road." Charing Cross was where the desert road branched north to Mersah Matruh. The Italian army was outside Mersah, and they were doing pretty well.

It was about the only time, so far as I know, that the Italians have done pretty well. Their morale goes up and down like a sensitive altimeter, and right then it was at forty thousand because the Axis was on top of the world. We hung around waiting for the refuelling to finish.

Peter said, "It's a piece of cake."

"Yes. It ought to be easy."

We separated and I climbed into my cockpit. I have always remembered the face of the airman who helped me to strap in. He was oldish, about forty, and bald except for a neat patch of golden hair at the back of his head. His face was all wrinkles, his eyes were like my grandmother's eyes, and he looked as though he had spent his life helping to strap in pilots who never came back. He stood on the wing pulling my straps and said, "Be careful. There isn't any sense not being careful."

"Piece of cake," I said.

"Like hell."

"Really. It isn't anything at all. It's a piece of cake."

I don't remember much about the next bit; I only remember about later on. I suppose we took off from Fouka and flew west towards Mersah, and I suppose we flew at about eight hundred feet. I suppose we saw the sea to starboard, and I suppose – no, I am certain – that it was blue and that it was beautiful, especially where it rolled up on to the sand and made a long thick white line east and west as far as you could see. I suppose we flew over Charing Cross and flew on for twenty-one miles to where they had said it would be, but I do not know. I know only that there was trouble, lots and lots of trouble, and I know that we had turned and were coming back when the trouble got worse. The biggest trouble of all was that I was too low to bale out, and it is from that point on that my memory comes back to me. I remember the dipping of the nose of the aircraft and I remember looking down the nose of the machine at the ground and seeing a little clump of camel-thorn growing there all by itself. I remember seeing some rocks lying in the sand beside the camel-thorn, and the camel-thorn and the sand and the rocks leapt out of the ground and came to me. I remember that very clearly.

Then there was a small gap of not-remembering. It might have been one second or it might have been thirty; I do not know. I have an idea that it was very short, a second perhaps, and next I heard a *crumph* on the right as the starboard wing tank caught fire, then another *crumph* on the left as the port tank did the same. To me that was not significant, and for a while I sat still, feeling comfortable, but a little drowsy. I couldn't see with my eyes, but that was not significant either. There was nothing to worry about. Nothing at all. Not until I felt the hotness around my legs. At first it was only a warmness and that was all right too, but all at once it was a hotness, a very stinging scorching hotness up and down the sides of each leg.

I knew that the hotness was unpleasant, but that was all I knew. I disliked it, so I curled my legs up under the seat and waited. I think there was something wrong with the telegraph system between the body and the brain. It did not seem to be working very well. Somehow it was a bit slow in telling the brain all about it and in asking for instructions. But I believe a message eventually got through, saying, "Down here there is a great hotness. What shall we do? (Signed) Left Leg and Right Leg." For a long time there was no reply. The brain was figuring the matter out.

Then slowly, word by word, the answer was tapped over the wires. "The – plane – is – burning. Get – out – repeat – get – out – get – out." The order was relayed to the whole system, to all the muscles in the legs, arms and body, and the muscles went to work. They tried their best; they pushed a little and pulled a little, and they strained greatly, but it wasn't any good. Up went another telegram, "Can't get out. Something holding us in." The answer to this one took even longer in arriving, so I just sat there waiting for it to come, and all the time the hotness increased. Something was holding me down and it was up to the brain to find out what it was. Was it giants' hands pressing on my shoulders, or heavy stones or houses or steam rollers or filing cabinets or gravity or was it ropes? Wait a minute. Ropes – ropes. The message was beginning to come through. It came very slowly. "Your – straps. Undo – your – straps." My arms received the message and went to work. They tugged at the straps, but they wouldn't undo. They tugged again and again, a little feebly, but as hard as they could, and it wasn't any use. Back went the message, "How do we undo the straps?"

This time I think that I sat there for three or four minutes waiting for the answer. It wasn't any use hurrying or getting impatient. That was the one thing of which I was sure. But what a long time it was all taking. I said aloud, "Bugger it. I'm going to be burnt. I'm . . ." but I was interrupted. The answer was coming – no, it wasn't – yes, it was, it was slowly coming through. "Pull – out – the – quick – release – pin – you – bloody – fool – and – hurry."

Out came the pin and the straps were loosed. Now, let's get out. Let's get out, let's get out. But I couldn't do it. I simply couldn't lift myself out of the cockpit. Arms and legs tried their best but it wasn't any use. A last desperate message was flashed upwards and this time it was marked "Urgent".

"Something else is holding us down," it said. "Something else, something else, something heavy."

Still the arms and legs did not fight. They seemed to know instinctively that there was no point in using up their strength. They stayed quiet and waited for the answer, and oh what a time it took. Twenty, thirty, forty hot seconds. None of them really white hot yet, no sizzling of flesh or smell of burning meat, but that would come any moment now, because those old Gladiators aren't made of stressed steel like a Hurricane or a Spit. They have taut canvas wings, covered with magnificently inflammable dope, and underneath there are hundreds of small thin sticks, the kind you put under the logs for kindling, only these are drier and thinner. If a clever man said, "I am going to build a big thing that will burn better and quicker than anything else in the world," and if he applied himself *diligently* to his task, he would probably finish up by building something very like a Gladiator. I sat still waiting.

Then suddenly the reply, beautiful in its briefness, but at the same time explaining everything. "Your – parachute – turn – the – buckle."

I turned the buckle, released the parachute harness and with some effort hoisted myself up and tumbled over the side of the cockpit. Something seemed to be burning, so I rolled about a bit in the sand, then crawled away from the fire on all fours and lay down.

I heard some of my machine-gun ammunition going off in the heat and I heard some of the bullets thumping into the sand nearby. I did not worry about them; I merely heard them.

Things were beginning to hurt. My face hurt most. There was something wrong with my face. Something had happened to it. Slowly I put up a hand to feel it. It was sticky. My nose didn't seem to be there. I tried to feel my teeth, but I cannot remember whether I came to any conclusion about them. I think I dozed off.

All of a sudden there was Peter. I heard his voice and I heard him dancing around and yelling like a madman and shaking my hand and saying, "Jesus, I thought you were still inside. I came down half a mile away and ran like hell. Are you all right?"

I said, "Peter, what has happened to my nose?"

I heard him striking a match in the dark. The night comes quickly in the desert. There was a pause.

"It actually doesn't seem to be there very much," he said. "Does it hurt?"

"Don't be a bloody fool, of course it hurts."

He said he was going back to his machine to get some morphia out of his emergency pack, but he came back again soon, saying he couldn't find his aircraft in the dark.

"Peter," I said, "I can't see anything."

"It's night," he answered. "I can't see either."

It was cold now. It was bitter cold, and Peter lay down close alongside so that we could both keep a little warmer. Every now and then he would say, "I've never seen a man without a nose before." I kept spewing a lot of blood and every time I did it, Peter lit a match. Once he gave me a cigarette, but it got wet and I didn't want it anyway.

I do not know how long we stayed there and I remember only very little more. I remember that I kept telling Peter that there was a tin of sore throat tablets in my pocket, and that he should take one, otherwise he would catch my sore throat. I remember asking him where we were and him saying, "We're between the two armies," and then I remember English voices from an English patrol asking if we were Italians. Peter said something to them; I cannot remember what he said.

Later I remember hot thick soup and one spoonful making me sick. And all the time the pleasant feeling that Peter was around, being wonderful, doing wonderful things and never going away. That is all that I can remember.

The men stood beside the aeroplane painting away and talking about the heat.

"Painting pictures on the aircraft," I said.

"Yes," said Peter. "It's a great idea. It's subtle."

"Why?" I said. "Just you tell me."

"They're funny pictures," he said. "The German pilots will all laugh when they see them; they'll shake so with their laughing that they won't be able to shoot straight."

"Oh baloney baloney baloney."

"No, it's a great idea. It's fine. Come and have a look."

We ran towards the line of aircraft. "Hop, skip, jump," said Peter. "Hop skip jump, keep in time."

"Hop skip jump," I said, "Hop skip jump," and we danced along.

The painter on the first aeroplane had a straw hat on his head and a sad face. He was copying the drawing out of a magazine, and when Peter saw it he said, "Boy oh boy look at that picture," and he began to laugh. His laugh began with a rumble and grew quickly into a belly-roar and he slapped his thighs with his hands both at the same time and went on laughing with his body doubled up and his mouth wide open and his eyes shut. His silk top hat fell off his head on to the sand.

"That's not funny," I said.

"Not funny!" he cried. "What d'you mean 'not funny'? Look at me. Look at me laughing. Laughing like this I couldn't hit anything. I couldn't hit a hay wagon or a house or a louse." And he capered about on the sand, gurgling and shaking with laughter. Then he seized me by the arm and we danced over to the next aeroplane. "Hop skip jump," he said. "Hop skip jump."

There was a small man with a crumpled face writing a long story on the fuselage with a red crayon. His straw hat was perched right on the back of his head and his head and his face was shiny with sweat.

"Good morning," he said. "Good morning, good morning," and he swept his hat off his head in a very elegant way.

Peter said, "Shut up," and bent down and began to read what the little man had been writing. All the time Peter was spluttering and rumbling with laughter, and as he read he began to laugh afresh. He rocked from one side to the other and danced around on the sand slapping his thighs with his hands and bending his body. "Oh my, what a story, what a story, what a story. Look at me. Look at me laughing," and he hopped about on his toes, shaking his head and chortling like a madman. Then suddenly I saw the joke and I began to laugh with him. I laughed so much that my stomach hurt and I fell down and rolled around on the sand and roared and roared because it was so funny that there was nothing else I could do.

"Peter, you're marvellous," I shouted. "But can all those German pilots read English?"

"Oh hell," he said. "Oh hell. Stop," he shouted. "Stop your work," and the painters all stopped their painting and turned round slowly and looked at Peter. They did a little caper on their toes and began to chant in unison.

"Rubbishy things – on all the wings, on all the wings, on all the wings," they chanted.

"Shut up," said Peter. "We're in a jam. We must keep calm. Where's my top hat?"

"What?" I said.

"You can speak German," he said. "You must translate for us. He will translate for you," he shouted to the painters. "He will translate."

Then I saw his black top hat lying in the sand. I looked away, then I looked around and saw it again. It was a silk opera hat and it was lying there on its side in the sand.

"You're mad," I shouted. "You're madder than hell. You don't know what you're doing. You'll get us all killed. You're absolutely plumb crazy, do you know that? You're crazier than hell. My God, you're crazy."

"Goodness, what a noise you're making. You mustn't shout like that; it's not good for you." This was a woman's voice. "You've made yourself all hot," she said, and I felt someone wiping my forehead with a handkerchief. "You mustn't work yourself up like that."

Then she was gone and I saw only the sky, which was pale blue. There were no clouds and all around were the German fighters. They were above, below and on every side and there was no way I could go; there was nothing I could do. They took it in turns to come in to attack and they flew their aircraft carelessly, banking and looping and dancing in the air. But I was not frightened, because of the funny pictures on my wings. I was confident and I thought, "I am going to fight a hundred of them alone and I'll shoot them all down. I'll shoot them while they are laughing; that's what I'll do."

Then they flew closer. The whole sky was full of them. There was so many that I did not know which ones to watch and which ones to attack. There were so many that they made a black curtain over the sky and only here and there could I see a little of the blue showing through. But there was enough to patch a Dutchman's trousers, which was all that mattered. So long as there was enough to do that, then everything was all right.

Still they flew closer. They came nearer and nearer, right up in front of my face so that I saw only the black crosses which stood out brightly against the colour of the Messerschmitts and against the blue of the sky; and as I turned my head quickly from one side to the other I saw more aircraft and more crosses and then I saw nothing but the arms of the crosses and the blue of the sky. The arms had hands and they joined together and made a circle and danced around my Gladiator, while the engines of the Messerschmitts sang joyfully in a deep voice. They were playing Oranges and Lemons and every now and then two would detach themselves and come out into the middle of the floor and make an attack and I knew then that it was Oranges and Lemons. They banked and swerved and danced upon their toes and they leant against the air first to one side, then to the other. "Oranges and Lemons said the bells of St Clement's," sang the engines.

But I was still confident. I could dance better than they and I had a better partner. She was the most beautiful girl in the world. I looked down and saw the curve of her neck and the gentle slope of her pale shoulders and I saw her slender arms, eager and outstretched.

Suddenly I saw some bullet holes in my starboard wing and I got angry. Then I got confident and I said, "The German who did that had no sense of humour. There's always one man in a party who has no sense of humour. But there's nothing to worry about; there's nothing at all to worry about."

Then I saw more bullet holes and I got scared. I slid back the hood of the cockpit and stood up and shouted, "You fools, look at the funny pictures. Look at the one on my tail; look at the story on my fuselage. Please look at the story on my fuselage."

But they kept on coming. They tripped into the middle of the floor in twos, shooting at me as they came. And the engines of the Messerschmitts sang loudly. "When will you pay me?

said the bells of Old Bailey," sang the engines, and as they sang the black crosses danced and swayed to the rhythm of the music. There were more holes in my wings, in the engine cowling and in the cockpit.

Then suddenly there were some in my body.

But there was no pain, even when I went into a spin, when the wings of my plane went flip, flip, flip, faster and faster, when the blue sky and the black sea chased each other round and round until there was no longer any sky or sea but just the flashing of the sun as I turned. But the black crosses were following me down, still dancing and still holding hands and I could still hear the singing of their engines. "Here comes a candle to light you to bed, here comes a chopper to chop off your head," sang the engines.

Still the wings went flip, flip, flip, flip, and there was neither sky nor sea around me, but only the sun.

Then there was only the sea. I could see it below me and I could see the white horses, and I said to myself, "Those are white horses riding a rough sea." I knew then that my brain was going well because of the white horses and because of the sea. I knew that there was not much time because the sea and the white horses were nearer, the white horses were bigger and the sea was like a sea and like water, not like a smooth place. Then there was only one white horse, rushing forward madly with his bit in his teeth, foaming at the mouth, scattering the spray with his hooves and arching his neck as he ran. He galloped on madly over the sea, riderless and uncontrollable, and I could tell that we were going to crash.

After that it was warmer, and there were no black crosses and there was no sky. But it was only warm because it was not hot and it was not cold. I was sitting in a great red chair made of velvet and it was evening. There was a wind blowing from behind.

"Where am I?" I said.

"You are missing. You are missing, believed killed."

"Then I must tell my mother."

"You can't. You can't use that phone."

"Why not?"

"It goes only to God."

"What did you say I was?"

"Missing, believed killed."

"That's not true. It's a lie. It's a lousy lie because here I am and I'm not missing. You're just trying to frighten me and you won't succeed. You won't succeed, I tell you, because I know it's a lie and I'm going back to my squadron. You can't stop me because I'll just go. I'm going, you see, I'm going."

I got up from the red chair and began to run.

"Let me see those X-rays again, nurse."

"They're here, doctor." This was the woman's voice again, and now it came closer. "You have been making a noise tonight, haven't you? Let me straighten your pillow for you, you're pushing it on to the floor." The voice was close and it was very soft and nice.

"Am I missing?"

"No, of course not. You're fine."

"They said I was missing."

"Don't be silly; you're fine."

Oh everyone's silly, silly, silly, but it was a lovely day, and I did not want to run but I couldn't stop. I kept on running across the grass and I couldn't stop because my legs were carrying me and I had no control over them. It was as if they did not belong to me, although when I looked down I saw that they were mine, that the shoes on the feet were mine and that the legs were joined to my body. But they would not do what I wanted; they just went on running across the field and I had to go with them. I ran and ran and ran, and although in some places the field was rough and bumpy, I never stumbled. I ran past trees and hedges and in one field there were some sheep which stopped their eating and scampered off as I ran past them. Once I saw my mother in a pale grey dress bending down picking mushrooms, and as I ran past she looked up and said, "My basket's nearly full; shall we go home soon?" but my legs wouldn't stop and I had to go on.

Then I saw the cliff ahead and I saw how dark it was beyond the cliff. There was this great cliff and beyond it there was nothing but darkness, although the sun was shining in the field where I was running. The light of the sun stopped dead at the edge of the cliff and there was only darkness beyond. "That must be where the night begins," I thought, and once more I tried to stop but it was not any good. My legs began to go faster towards the cliff and they began to take longer strides, and I reached down with my hand and tried to stop them by clutching the cloth of my trousers, but it did not work; then I tried to fall down. But my legs were nimble, and each time I threw myself I landed on my toes and went on running.

Now the cliff and the darkness were much nearer and I could see that unless I stopped quickly I should go over the edge. Once more I tried to throw myself to the ground and once more I landed on my toes and went on running.

I was going fast as I came to the edge and I went straight on over it into the darkness and began to fall.

At first it was not quite dark. I could see little trees growing out of the face of the cliff, and I grabbed at them with my hands as I went down. Several times I managed to catch hold of a branch, but it always broke off at once because I was so heavy and because I was falling so fast, and once I caught a thick branch with both hands and the tree leaned forward and I heard the snapping of the roots one by one until it came away from the cliff and I went on falling. Then it became darker because the sun and the day were in the fields far away at the top of the cliff, and as I fell I kept my eyes open and watched the darkness turn from grey-black to black, from black to jet black and from jet black to pure liquid blackness which I could touch with my hands but which I could not see. But I went on falling, and it was so black that there was nothing anywhere and it was not any use doing anything or caring or thinking because of the blackness and because of the falling. It was not any use.

"You're better this morning. You're much better." It was the woman's voice again.

"Hallo."

"Hallo; we thought you were never going to get conscious."

"Where am I?"

"In Alexandria; in hospital."

"How long have I been here?"

"Four days."

"What time is it?"

"Seven o'clock in the morning."

"Why can't I see?"

I heard her walking a little closer.

"Oh, we've just put a bandage around your eyes for a bit."

"How long for?"

"Just for a while. Don't worry. You're fine. You were very lucky, you know."

I was feeling my face with my fingers but I couldn't feel it; I could only feel something else.

"What's wrong with my face?"

I heard her coming up to the side of my bed and I felt her hand touching my shoulder.

"You mustn't talk any more. You're not allowed to talk. It's bad for you. Just lie still and don't worry. You're fine."

I heard the sound of her footsteps as she walked across the floor and I heard her open the door and shut it again.

"Nurse," I said. "Nurse."

But she was gone.

Points for Discussion and Suggestions for Writing

1 Which is your favourite story? Write a brief review which would persuade another reader to try Roald Dahl for the first time.
2 Does this selection of stories tell you anything about the writer's likes and dislikes?
3 Do you think Roald Dahl is suggesting that animals are cleverer or wiser than people? Have you ever believed, or do you believe this to be the case? Which characteristics of animals does Dahl seem to value?
4 Do you feel particularly drawn to any of the people in these stories? Try to describe in more detail the personality and attitudes of at least one character.
5 F. Scott Fitzgerald wrote a story called "The beautiful and the damned". Which of Dahl's characters could be described as beautiful or damned?
6 Many of Dahl's characters are people with obsessions, for example, the two boys in *The Swan* are obsessed with killing, Lexington in *Pig* is obsessed with food, and Albert in *Royal Jelly* is obsessed with bees. Are there any connexions drawn between these characters?

The Swan

1 "Brought up in a household where physical violence was an everyday occurrence, he was himself an extremely violent person." What kinds of violence does Ernie practise? Why do you think he is violent?
2 "Peter Watson was always the enemy." Do you think that Peter sees Ernie and Raymond as the "enemy"? Did Peter dislike them because they were nearly everything he was not?
3 "Perisher", "twerp", "bleeder", "squirt", "lout", "snotty-nose", "hooligan". Do you use any of these

terms? Can you think of any more? What kind of atmosphere do they produce?

4 Peter's father reads a newspaper everyday. Ernie's father "was already slouching on the sofa watching the telly at nine-thirty on this Saturday morning".

What do these two pieces of information tell us about the boys' fathers? What kind of relationship do you think Peter has with his father? And Ernie? Do you think their mothers have much influence on them?

5 How does Dahl achieve the effect of the speeding train?

6 "All he could do therefore, was to keep calm and try to talk his way out of the situation." Do you think that this was the best decision? What would you have done?

7 Write a fuller account of Peter's schoolday experiences.

8 Which of the three boys knows the most about fear in this story? How has he learned so much?

9 "How much further could this madness go? Peter wondered. He was beginning to feel a little mad himself, as though nothing was real anymore and none of it was actually happening." Is the ending of this story part of that madness? Or is it magic?

Pig

1 "Once upon a time in the city of New York, a beautiful baby boy was born into this world, and the joyful parents named him Lexington." How does this beginning effect the way in which we read the story?

2 How is Aunt Glosspan responsible for what happens to Lexington?

3 Towards the end of the story, Dahl several times refers to Lexington as "our hero". Why do you think he does this? Isn't Lexington always "our hero"?

4 "One lives and learns" says the waiter. How would you describe the kind of life Lexington lives? What does he learn? Does it amount to anything significant?

5 McPottle, Lexington, Glosspan, Zuckermann. Why does Dahl use so many unusual names in this story? What do they bring to the narrative?

6 Why does Lexington lose most of the money?

7 "Why, it's downright subversive," says Mr Zuckermann when Lexington tells how he buried his aunt's body.

Why doesn't Lexington respond to this comment? Do you think he knows what Zuckermann means?

8 "He travelled on foot, and he slept under hedges, and he lived on berries and wild herbs, and it took him sixteen days to reach the metropolis."
Write a fuller description of how Lexington survived during those sixteen days.

9 Reading, writing, geography, arithmetic and cooking were the five subjects in which Aunt Glosspan provided lessons for Lexington. What are the advantages and disadvantages of this choice of subjects?

The Boy Who Talked With Animals

1 In what ways do we begin to sense that there is "danger in paradise"? Do you think the narrator was really looking for trouble?

2 Are the taxi-driver and the house-maid being friendly when they talk to him? What do you think they feel about tourists?

3 "Many of the women were squealing with pleasure clutching on to the arms of their men, and the men were demonstrating their lack of fear and their masculinity by making foolish remarks in loud voices." Is this a fair comment on sex roles?

4 Whose side are you on in the dispute over the turtle? Why?

5 How are the other tourists described by the narrator? Sketch a description of the narrator.

6 Why do the men who are pulling the turtle stop when they hear the child scream?

7 "The voice of the boy's mother, the stricken, agonized wail of the mother's voice rose up in the evening sky."
Why does the mother cry out like this? Does the description remind you of anything?

8 "He loves animals," the father said, "He really loves them. He communicates with them." Is this a satisfactory definition of love?

9 "Something had happened. Something strange had come fluttering across the beach." Is there any other way of describing that "something"?

10 Is the ending of this story believable? Compare it with the ending of *The Swan*.

The Wish

1 How does Roald Dahl suggest the age of this child? How old do you think he is? Would the child play the same game if it were female?

2 Do you remember playing this kind of game? How long did it take? Try to describe the rules you made and what happened in the game.

3 There are three colours in the carpet – red, black and yellow. With what feelings does the child associate those colours? Why do you think this is so?

4 Imagine that you are the child and mother opens the front door. What would your reactions be? How would you feel?

5 How might we guess that this child plays alone often? What other games do you think he would enjoy?

6 Why does the author tell us that the child's mother is "outside in the sunshine"?

7 How does Dahl create tension in this story?

8 It is acknowledged that children are most at risk while they are in their own homes. Where is the risk of danger for this child?

9 Write a fuller description of the hallway and the house.

The Way Up To Heaven

1 "He had disciplined her too well for that. He must also have known that if he was prepared to wait even beyond the last moment of safety, he could drive her nearly into hysterics. On one or two occasions in the later years of their married life, it seemed as though he had wanted to miss the train simply in order to intensify the poor woman's suffering."

What does this tell us about Mr Foster's character? Do you think he really likes his wife?

2 "Mrs Foster was and always had been a good and loving wife. For over thirty years, she had served him loyally and well."

What is Dahl suggesting about the relationship between these two married people?

3 Why do you think Mrs Foster wanted so much to be close to her grandchildren? Describe her meeting with them.

4 A "quick clever old squirrel from the Park" is one example of the animal imagery used to describe Mr Foster. Can you find some other examples? What effect does using this kind of imagery have on the story?

5 "The eyes never showed anything except when he was in a rage." Does Mr Foster deserve what he gets? Do you think there is some kind of justice in the ending?

6 Describe the relationship you imagine existed between Mr Foster and his daughter.

7 "She felt remarkably strong, and in a queer sort of way, wonderful." Why does Mrs Foster now feel strong and wonderful?

Royal Jelly

1 "A little knowledge is a dangerous thing." Albert knows about bees. Does he know enough? Is the way in which he uses his knowledge dangerous?

2 What were Mabel's thoughts and feelings? Write your own version of the mother's story with her as the central character.

3 Imagine that Albert wrote about this experience in an article to send to *Beecraft*, one of the magazines he reads. What records would he need to keep? How would he keep them? What might he demonstrate? Do you think readers would be interested in what he had to say?

4 How would you describe the relationship between Albert and Mabel Taylor? How does it compare with that of the Fosters in *The Way Up To Heaven*?

5 ". . . sometimes he would put them on his face and let them crawl about over his cheeks and neck, and the astonishing thing about it all was that he never got stung." Do you think that this could really happen to anyone? Why?

6 This is the kind of story that can frustrate a reader since it seems to finish too soon. Can you imagine another ending which frustrates less, but still leaves quite a bit up in the air?

7 In another story, *The Ratcatcher*, Dahl makes the main

character look and seem like a rat. Albert Taylor's "head was huge and round, covered with bristly short-cut hair, and the greater part of the face ... was hidden by a brownish yellow fuzz about an inch long." What do these stories gain by having animal-like or insect-like humans in them? Do we learn more about the animals or the people?

Poison

1 Look at this story from a different point of view. How do you think Dr Ganderbai would relate his evening to a friend?

2 Since this story is told by Timber Woods, we do not have much information about him other that what we glean from his actions and responses regarding his friend Harry and Dr Ganderbai. Describe what kind of person you think he is.

3 Do you think there ever was a krait in the bed, or was Harry playing a joke on his friend? Why does Dr Ganderbai say what he does at the end?

4 When this story was televised in the series "Tales of the Unexpected", several changes were made. Timber gained a girlfriend who, fed up with little attention from Timber, drove away in Dr Ganderbai's car. Do you think that this story needs extra "spice" to make it more interesting, or does the plot as it is hold the reader's interest?

5 "By the time you get there I will have waked up my boy on the telephone and he will show you my poisons cupboard. Here is the key of the cupboard. Take a bottle of chloroform. It has an orange label and the name is printed on it. I stay here in case anything happens. Be quick now, hurry! No, no, you don't need your shoes." Very subtly, Dahl indicates in this speech that the speaker is not English. How does he do this?

6 "It is odd how one sometimes has frivolous thoughts at exciting moments and I distinctly remember thinking about Harry being very refined when I saw that button." Here we are waiting to find out whether or not there is a snake on Harry's stomach, and we are stopped by this observation. Does it add to the tension or not? How?

A Piece of Cake – my first story – 1942

1 What do you know about being a fighter pilot in World War II after reading this piece? Does it bear any relation to other description or images you may have from cinema or history?

2 "I do not remember much of it; not beforehand anyway; not until it happened." What happened? What is this "it" Dahl refers to?

3 How can we tell when the narrator is conscious and when he is unconscious? What devices does Dahl use to make this shift?

4 "The biggest trouble of all was that I was too low to bail out, and it is from this point on that my memory comes back to me." Why does his memory came back clearly at this point?

5 This story shows how we remember in patches. Can you describe in detail exactly what happened to and around you in the hour before you read this story?

6 Are there enough facts and detail provided for another person to write a description of the experience of being shot down? Imagine you are Peter writing a letter home.

7 "But there was enough to patch a Dutchman's trousers, which was all that mattered. So long as there was enough to do that, then everything was all right." What does this mean?

Wider reading – selected authors

You might like to read the work of others who write both for children and older readers. These are not necessarily the best, but you may already have read some of their stories for children and not know what else they write. It may be interesting to try to identify whether they use different styles or voices depending on the target audience.

BANKS, LYNNE REID
Backward shadow, Penguin.
Children at the gate, Penguin.
An end to running, Penguin.
The L-shaped room, Penguin.
Two is lonely, Penguin.

BAWDEN, NINA
The ice house, Macmillan.
Afternoon of a good woman, Macmillan.
Familiar passions, Macmillan.
The birds on the trees, Penguin.

DICKINSON, PETER
Skin deep, Hamlyn publications.
A pride of heroes, Hamlyn publications.
Sleep and his brother, Hamlyn publications.

LIVELY, PENELOPE
Next to nature, art, Heinemann.
Judgement day, Heinemann.
Nothing missing but the samovar, and other stories, Heinemann.
Revenge of Samuel Stokes, Heinemann.
Road to Lichfield, Heinemann.

Wider reading – short stories

"Not that the story need be long, but it will take a long while to make it short." Thoreau

Some of us prefer to read short stories, especially when the time available for continuous reading is limited, when we are unable to commit ourselves to a novel for reasons of work, study or exhaustion. They are ideal for the journey to school or work, while waiting for someone else to cook, while waiting in the health centre, or even as a satisfying diversion from that novel which is going on and on. They are a very different kind of reading experience. Some writers of short stories compress complicated ideas into very small packages.

Patricia Highsmith's *Little tales of mysogny* retell familiar fairy tales in a few pages, and Fay Weldon's *Gift of Life*, a salutory fable, horrifies, offends, and instructs in four hundred words! The short story facilitates development of close examination of what happens in a small slice of life, as though through a microscope, or in a snapshot, or reflected in a convex mirror. Often we hear someone say "you can't see the wood for the trees", a remark which only underlines the main problem, that is, the way in which we look at the trees. Short stories provide good training in perception, learning *how* to look at the trees in order to see the wood.

The following list of authors has been chosen because they are so varied. It is a very personal choice from a short story addict.

COPPARD, A. E. *Dusty Ruth and other stories*, Penguin, 1974.

HIGHSMITH, PATRICIA *Little tales of mysogny*, Penguin, 1980.

HERLIHY, JAMES LEO *The sleep of Baby Filbertson and other stories*, Penguin, 1964.

LIM, CATHERINE *Little stories of Singapore*, Heinemann educational books, 1978.

McCULLERS, CARSON *The ballad of the sad cafe*, Penguin, 1963.

MAUCHAM, W. SOMERSET *Collected short stories, vol. 4*, Pan, 1976.

SILLITOE, ALAN *Men, women, and children*, W. H. Allen, 1975.

TREVOR, WILLIAM *Lovers of their time and other stories*, Bodley Head, Stories Penguin, 1983.

WELDON, FAY *Polaris, and other short stories*, Hodder and Stoughton, 1985.

NANDY, PRITISH,ed. *The Vikas book of modern Indian love stories*, Vikas publishing, 1979.

PALEY, GRACE *Enormous changes at the last minute*, Virago, 1979. *Little disturbances of man*, Virago, 1980.

MARLAND, MICHAEL, ed. *Short stories for today*, Longman Study Texts, 1984. *The experience of love*, Longman Imprint Books, 1980. *Meetings and partings*, Longman Imprint Books, 1984.

HEALY, MAURA, ed. *Women*, Longman Imprint Books, 1985.

GIBBS, ANNA & TILSON, ALISON, eds. *Frictions: and anthology of fiction by women*, Sybylla cooperative press and publications, 1982.

BINDING, T. J. ed. *Firebird, 2: writing today*, Penguin, 1983.

SALKEY, ANDREW, ed. *West Indian stories*, Faber and Faber, 1960.

MARQUEZ, GABRIEL GARCIA *Leaf storm and other stories*, Trans. from the Spanish by Gregory Rabassa, Cape, 1972.

RIVE, RICHARD, ed. *Modern African prose; an anthology*, Heinemann, 1973.

BELLOW, SAUL *Mosby's memoirs and other stories*, Weidenfeld and Nicolson, 1969.

Modern Arabic short stories, selected and translated by Denys Johnson-Davies, Heinemann, 1967.

DUGGAL, K. S. *Come back, My Master, and other stories*, Bell books, 1979.

WASHINGTON, MARY HELEN ed. *Any woman's blues: stories by contemporary black woman writers*, Virago, 1980.

WELDON, FAY *The gift of life*, in Fiction magazine, Vol. 2 no. 2. Autumn, 1983.

Further reading – Roald Dahl

Roald Dahl's Book of ghost stories, Cape, 1983.

Boy, Cape, 1983.

A Roald Dahl selection, ed. Roy Blatchford, Longman Imprint Books, 1980.

Kiss, kiss, Penguin, 1969.

More tales of the unexpected, Penguin, 1980.

My Uncle Oswald, Penguin, 1980.
Over to you, Penguin, 1973.
Revolting rhymes, Penguin, 1984.
Someone like you, Penguin, 1970.
Switch bitch, Penguin, 1976.
Tales of the unexpected, Penguin, 1979.
Taste and other tales, Longman, 1979.
The way up to heaven, and other stories, Murray, 1981. (English easy readers)
The witches, Cape, 1983.
The wonderful story of Henry Sugar and six more, Penguin, 1982.

Longman Imprint Books
General Editor: Michael Marland CBE MA